A Scottish Christmas Dream

JENNIFER NICE

eBook: 978-1-912903-45-0
Paperback: 978-1-912903-46-7
Large Print: 978-1-912903-47-4

Cover design and typesetting by
Write into the Woods.

www.writeintothewoods.com

Books By
JENNIFER NICE

Christmas At The Manor:
Merry Christmas Eve Eve
That's It In A Nutcracker
All's Fair In Love And Christmas

**The Nice Romance Collection
(a series of standalone romances):**
Digging the Director
A Scottish Christmas Dream
Let's Skip This Christmas
Yellow Petals At Christmas

Join the
CLUB

Find all of the above books and sign up to the mailing
list for more at
www.writeintothewoods.com/romance

For my mum.
Thank you for all our wonderful Edinburgh
adventures.

A LIVING ROOM
SOMEWHERE IN
EDINBURGH...

'I call this New Moon meeting of the Weird Reading Sisters to order,' said Doreen. 'Did anyone actually read the book?' She poured wine into each of their glasses.

'Of course not. What a load of tripe,' said Faye, slamming the book onto the coffee table between them and picking up her glass.

'Oh, I did,' said Molly. 'I thought it was wonderful.'

Faye raised an eyebrow.

'Had a happy ending, did it?'

Molly nodded.

'The detective solved the murder.' She leaned forward, taking up her wine glass and whispering, 'It was the son that did it.' She leaned back, sipping at the wine. Faye watched her.

'Well, now I don't need to read it, do I.' She took a gulp of her own drink.

'I got halfway through before I got bored,'

Doreen admitted. 'How about you, Esme?'

Esme Munro peered at each of her friends in turn and then shrugged, lifting her glass to her lips and taking a long pull at the wine.

'I read it in one day. It was predictable but well written. Can we have something other than crime next time?'

The other women nodded in agreement, although Molly appeared a little less eager than the others.

'Right, then. Down to business,' said Doreen, sitting back with her own glass. 'What troubles are you each bringing to the table, girls? Faye. You go first.'

Faye placed down her glass and brushed her hands together, leaning forward and straightening out the skirt of her dress over her knees.

'Last month I told you how my granddaughter was suffering from the night terrors,' she started. Each woman sitting around the coffee table on the sofa and in armchairs nodded. 'I smudged the house with sage, as was suggested, and the very next night, the terrors stopped. They haven't come back.' Faye smiled. 'This month I have nothing to report other than a happy granddaughter and for that, I am truly grateful for each of you.'

The women raised their glasses to one another and drank deep. Doreen refilled each glass in turn.

'Molly?'

Molly swallowed her wine and leaned forward.

'My friends, I am having a problem with getting someone out to look at my boiler. My usual man is away and it's been two days since I had hot water. Everyone I try either doesn't pick up their phone or says they'll come round but then don't. It's as if every plumber in the city doesn't want the work.' Molly huffed. 'What should I do?'

'Easy,' said Faye. 'My son-in-law has recently started his own plumbing and gas business. You should have told me earlier.' She tutted, taking a pen and old receipt from her purse. Leaning forward, she scribbled numbers onto the paper. 'I'll tell him to expect your call and if he doesn't do the job tomorrow then I'll give him a clout around the ear.' Faye handed the number to Molly, who grinned.

'Oh, thank you, Faye.'

They each raised their glasses to one another and sipped their wine.

'Doreen?' asked Esme.

Doreen sat back, inhaling deeply, searching for the right words.

'I want Howard to ask me to dance at the next ballroom class.'

There was a pause and then the women broke down into giggles.

'Why don't you ask him yourself?' Faye pondered, taking the bottle and emptying it into her glass.

'Because I want him to ask me,' repeated Doreen.

'Howard's a shy one,' Molly told her. 'He'll need

a nudge.'

They glanced at one another, silently discussing who would be the nudger in this instance. Once decided, all four raised their glasses and drank their wine.

'I have a similar issue,' said Esme. 'Although I don't think it can be fixed in the same way.'

'Do tell,' said Molly as Doreen opened another bottle and topped up their glasses. 'I don't think you've ever mentioned being interested in a man since your Jim passed.'

Esme gave a sad smile.

'It's not me,' she told them. 'It's my son. My youngest. Michael. He took over his father's work and done my Jim proud. He's worked so hard all his life and while he won't admit to it, I can tell he's lonely. Oh, he has friends, sure, but he can't be with them all the time. To be his age and still get into a cold bed each night. Friends, I want my youngest to find what I had at his age, what his brother has found. I want him to find love.'

A silence descended over the coffee table. This wasn't such an easy fix.

'I remember years ago, we tried to set Michael up with my great-niece,' said Molly. 'It didn't go well.'

'They were a good match, as well,' Faye confirmed. 'What went wrong?'

'She told me she couldn't compete with his work.'

The women sagged, staring down into their full

4

wine glasses.

'There's nothing else for it, then,' said Doreen, glancing up.

'Indeed. Nothing else,' said Faye, sitting up straighter.

'We'll have to ask the Universe,' agreed Molly.

Doreen pulled herself from her chair and stepped over to the bookcase. Running her finger over the spines, she found the book she wanted, pulled it out and fell back into her chair.

'Here,' she said, finding the right page. 'A request to the Universe. We don't need much. I think I have most of these. Drink up, girls. Tonight, we'll be doing a spell.'

The four women toasted the news and downed their wine in one.

One

'Are you sure about this?'

Frankie glanced back to her mother with a stupid grin on her face and then gestured to the dilapidated hallway in front of them.

'Of course! Look at it. It's going to be beautiful.'

Irene wasn't convinced. She pulled a face and slid some of the dirt on the floor along with her shoe.

'It's a lot of work, Frankie. More than I remember. Was it this bad when we viewed it?'

'Yup.'

'Hmm. Aren't there companies who just come in and renovate houses? I'm sure there are.'

'No, Mum.' Frankie turned on her mother and made sure Irene was looking her in the eye. 'I'm doing this myself.' She grinned again, unable to keep it away for long. 'It'll be fine. I've done this before.'

Irene blew out her cheeks.

'Not on this scale. A little Victorian terrace isn't

quite the same.'

With her back turned, Frankie rolled her eyes.

'That little Victorian terrace was a menace. A little Victorian terrace menace,' said Frankie, running her hand over the ornate banister and glancing up the stairs. The carpet was threadbare and, quite frankly, disgusting. But rip the carpet up, give the wood a sand and a coat of varnish, paint the stairs, fix the panelling, and it would be glorious. 'I can do this. It'll take me a while, but come on' – she looked back to her mother – 'what else am I going to do?'

Irene had no answer, so she hugged herself and sighed.

A sharp bark caught both their attention and Irene looked out of the open front door to the sweeping, weed-laden gravel driveway. Frankie appeared beside her.

Her father was directing a large removals lorry into the driveway while simultaneously holding back their toffee-coloured cocker spaniel. Lily was up on her back legs, straining against Geoff's hold on her collar, eager to tell the removal lorry exactly what she thought of it.

Frankie clapped her hands and strode out into the cold Scottish winter sunshine to welcome the moving men.

'Where are they going to put all your stuff?' came Irene's voice, following her out. 'Nowhere's ready.'

'I'll shove it all in the back rooms for now,' Frankie called back. 'I'll be doing those rooms last.'

Irene took the dog from her husband and stood back to watch father and daughter greet and direct the four moving men, who were surprisingly chirpy for having driven from London to the Scottish Borders and now had to lug furniture around.

Geoff organised where his and Irene's belongings were placed in the cottage beside the main house before stretching, hands on the small of his back. Then, Frankie guided the men, moving boxes and furniture into the large farmhouse. Her father regularly tried to take over and eventually her mother dragged the dog into their cottage to hunt down the kettle.

All of Frankie's belongings were squeezed into two rooms; one upstairs and one downstairs. She'd spend some evenings sorting them out as she went along. With the last box, full of kitchen items, delivered, Frankie showed the men over to the cottage where Irene was waiting for tea orders.

'I'm afraid there's no cake.'

One of the men laughed.

'That's all right. Just tea would be great, and then we need to get going.'

They all murmured their appreciation and stood around the small kitchen, sipping from their cups. One crouched, ruffling Lily's ears.

'It's a big, old place,' said the man in charge to Geoff. Frankie's father gestured to his daughter.

'It's all her doing. She wanted to move to Scotland, buy a project and decided she'd like us to tag along.'

All eyes turned to Frankie and she wilted a little. Shrugging, she looked past them all to the tiny courtyard that constituted the garden of the cottage.

'I needed an adventure.'

'Needs a lot of work,' said the man, glancing around the kitchen.

'Yeah, but nothing we can't handle,' Frankie explained. 'I want to make sure Mum and Dad are happy, especially as I've dragged them all this way. We're hopefully building an extension on the side' – she pointed – 'to double the size of this kitchen. Otherwise it's all cosmetic. The previous owners built this as a holiday cottage for extra income but were living here after the main house became too much to handle, so it's not too bad.'

'Garden needs sorting, too,' said the man pointedly.

Frankie puffed out her cheeks.

'Given how big the main house's garden is, I told Dad we'd knock down the separating wall and he could choose how much of a garden he wanted.'

The man laughed.

'Well, I guess he's paying for it all. And you get the big house, huh?'

Frankie stiffened and her mother pursed her lips.

'Actually, she's paying for everything,' said Geoff. 'With cash. She's a savvy one, my girl. Got herself a career in Hollywood, making big films, invested the money wisely in London and has now bought her dream home. Plus she's going to do most of the work herself. I'm just here to enjoy my retirement and grow vegetables.' He sniffed and sipped his tea.

Frankie swallowed hard as, once again, all eyes turned to her. The man crouching, cuddling the dog, looked her up and down.

'Making big films?' one of them asked. 'You a fancy director or something?'

'Or something,' Frankie murmured. 'Actor,' she clarified. 'But I've quit that now.'

'Retired,' her mother corrected.

The men were still looking at her. Frankie sighed.

'I'm Francesca Taylor. The Defenders movies, surely you've seen those?'

They squinted, narrowing their eyes, trying to place her.

'I played the teleporter.'

One of them frowned.

'As in, she could teleport from one place to another?' Frankie tried. 'She left a puff of smoke behind each time. Roxie Black. Her superhero name is Smoke. No?'

One of them starting laughing, snapping his fingers at her.

'Oh god, you're Roxie Black! I didn't recognise you without the silver hair. But I see it now. Is that a wig you have to wear?'

'Yeah, great fun in sweltering L.A. heat,' Frankie told him, a touch of a smile on her lips.

'Not porn, then,' one of the men murmured, just loud enough for her mother to flinch.

'No.' Frankie stared at him until his cheeks flushed and he turned away.

'You must be worth millions,' said the man stroking Lily, looking around the cottage with new wonder in his eyes.

'Not as much as people think. I'm not a big name. As you've all just proven. People think I got paid a lot more for those films than I did.'

'But you've got enough to buy all of this with cash.'

'Well, yeah—'

'But she's doing all the work herself,' said the man in charge with a sniff. 'Good luck with that. We best be off, boys. Drink up. Thank you for the tea. Have fun settling in.' He smiled at Irene and Geoff, and gave Frankie a look as he passed her.

Frankie waited until the lorry had left the driveway before she sagged.

'No! Nope! Don't you dare!' cried Irene, rushing over and placing a hand on her daughter's back. 'Don't let them get to you. Remember, you retired from all that for a reason. Now is the beginning of something new. And look at where we are. There are hills over there! With snow on them already! And Edinburgh is just down the road. No more having to figure out flights or train timetables just for a weekend away. We can just pop in whenever we like.'

It worked, the big grin returning to Frankie's face.

'Yeah,' she murmured. 'You're right. Yes. Let's get cracking, shall we? Where shall we start?'

'What should I mark out the garden with?' asked Geoff, plonking his tea mug down and smacking his lips. 'Lily can help me.'

Frankie laughed.

'Sure, okay. I'll let you out the back door in the farmhouse. I need to try the key, hang on.' She dug into her pocket for the keys the estate agent had given her. 'Mum? What do you want to do?'

'I should start unpacking, really,' Irene murmured, looking at the stacked boxes.

'Not if you don't want to,' said Frankie.

'Got all retirement for that,' Geoff pointed out.

Irene smiled.

'Good point. Okay, let's go explore the big house. Tell me your plans.'

The women squealed with glee and Frankie led the way out of the cottage and across the driveway.

'And then maybe we can have a look at things we can do in Edinburgh,' Frankie offered, their feet crunching over the gravel.

'Will you have time? You've got so much work to do on the houses,' said her mother.

Frankie gave her a look.

'We could look for things for you to do.'

Irene gave a broad smile, which fell as they stepped into the farmhouse, through the wreck that was the kitchen, where Frankie attempted to unlock the back door.

'Oh, we need to register Lily at the local vets. She's due her booster shot, too. That'll be a good way of getting to know the vet. And the town, I guess,' Irene said gently, looking around the room.

The back door opened with a jolt and a creak. Lily was out immediately, racing around with her nose to the grass. Frankie found a can of spray paint in a nearby box. The removal company had refused to bring all of her leftover paint from her last project, citing that paint could explode in the warm temperatures of the lorry, despite the chill that came as November turned to December, so the box had travelled up with Frankie in her car.

'Here, put a line where you want the new fence to go.' She handed the can to her father and he left, smiling gleefully and shaking the can.

'I can call the vets, if you like?'

'Frankie.' Her mother tutted. 'You don't have to do everything for us. I'll give them a call and make an appointment. But first, tell me what you're going to do and where. Paint me a picture of how beautiful this place is going to be.'

Frankie's heart skipped and she took a moment to appreciate the thrill of happiness. It had been a while since her body had reacted in such a way.

'I'm going to knock down the middle of this wall,' she started, gesturing at the wall between the kitchen and dining room. 'One big kitchen diner.'

'Lovely.'

'And I'll rip this kitchen out, replace it with cabinets all along this wall.'

'What colour will they be?'

'Blue.'

'Oh, like the Victorian terrace menace in London.'

'Yeah. I kind of wish I could have brought that kitchen with me.'

Irene laughed and led the way out of the kitchen and into the hallway, Frankie followed, gazing around, seeing the house exactly as she wanted it.

Two

As the city of Edinburgh woke, just before seven thirty, a row of Victorian townhouses listened to the soft notes of a piano being played. This wasn't uncommon. It happened most mornings since Michael Munro had purchased the top floor flat of one particular converted Victorian townhouse and had managed to put a piano in the sitting room. The delivery men hadn't been happy to lug the piano up the stairs, but Michael had ensured they were paid extra and that tea and biscuits were waiting for them at the top. He had no idea how he was going to get the piano out if he ever moved. He often considered whether he'd leave it there for the new owners and treat himself to a grand piano that couldn't be heaved up Victorian staircases.

Whenever and wherever that was.

Moving was often something Michael threatened himself with. He would move to the countryside and buy a period building to bring back to life, or an old farmhouse that he could fill with rescue animals, or perhaps he would eventually give in, marry a woman his friends would introduce him to and buy an executive new build on an estate filled with identical executive new builds.

No, that wouldn't happen. He wouldn't let it.

He sighed as his long fingers danced over the piano keys, his travel mug of coffee steaming on the table behind him, waiting patiently. On top of the piano, Agnes lay curled up, peering out of the window and purring along with the piano's vibrations.

Michael's mind wandered as he played. He often found himself in a good mood, and this particular one seemed to have sprung from a dream he'd had that night. Michael didn't dream much and when he did, it was usually because of a bad day, when grief and horror needed processing. This dream, however, had been pleasant. More than pleasant. Which was why he replayed it as he played the piano, giving his dream its own soundtrack. Revisiting the images his brain had conjured of meeting a woman, of talking with her, of kissing her, slipping her dress straps from her shoulders. Her warmth and soft skin had been so real, he could still feel them under his fingertips and on his lips. Her long dark hair had been brushed away to reveal her bare shoulders which he'd kissed softly. She'd smelled of the out-side, of the breeze and water and grass. Her large eyes had been captivating and soft, while her lips had urged him on.

It had been a long time since Michael had dreamed anything like that and never had a dream been so vivid.

He wasn't going to question where it had come from or what it meant, he was just going to enjoy reliving it, over and over.

When the piece ended, Michael sat back and took a moment to smile as the city noises made their way into hearing. Then he finished getting ready for work, put the lid on his coffee and locked his front door behind him.

The dream of moving to the countryside was what had made him buy the practice outside of the city. His father had left him the family's city veterinary practice, which Michael had thrown himself into, growing it in directions he hoped his father would be proud of. It was another vet who had told him about the practice coming up for sale in Bekburn.

Michael liked to think that he gave all of his business decisions a great deal of consideration, however, his mind had already been made up about the purchase before he consulted his mother on what his father would have wanted.

'Stop it,' she'd told him. 'This is your business now. And if you're yearning for fields then go be out in the fields.'

It had probably been a flippant remark, but Michael's brain had taken that statement and stored it away, bringing it out whenever his bones started to grow tired of the city.

By eight o'clock, he was driving out of Edinburgh. It wasn't a long drive, as such, but getting out of the city could be a hassle. Once out, the drive usually took around forty-five minutes, so Michael sat back, sipped his coffee and listened to the radio until he hit the main road and was able to pick up speed.

The small town of Bekburn was everything Michael dreamed of when he thought of moving to the countryside, unless he was having one of those days when he considered moving to the rugged west coast or maybe down to England. It was quaint, picturesque, with delicate architecture and period homes in the centre. New developments flanked the outskirts, but that was okay because trees lined most of the roads. Despite new large supermarkets springing up, the centre of the town and its high street still had that atmosphere of somewhere far away, somewhere hidden, an escape, and an echo of times when people worked in factories and on the farms rather than behind computers. There were small parks where the river rushed through and families played on the grass and on swings and slides. If you stood outside the main entrance to Michael's veterinary practice and looked right, you would see a wonderfully green view of trees lining the top of hills and fields stretched between the town and the highest vantage point. Except for this time of year, when snow lay over the hills and the trees were becoming bare and stark against the brown landscape.

Michael hummed as he parked his car and carried his bag and empty coffee cup to the high street. The local council had only recently put the finishing touches to the town's Christmas decorations. Mini potted trees lined the high street festooned with lights, currently switched off in the morning glow, and more lights swung between the buildings, across the road. At the top of the high street stood a magnificent spruce, tastefully decorated, ready to light up the town centre as the sun dipped behind the hills. There was just enough room around the tree for carollers and space had been roped off for a charity table where volunteers accepted gifts and parcels each weekend. Michael breathed in the clear countryside air, looked at the view of the hills and then pushed open the main door to his practice.

'Good morning, boss!'

'Good morning, Sandy. How are you? Everything all right?'

His receptionist nodded as she took a sip of her coffee and gave him a thumbs up. He'd inherited most of the staff when he'd purchased the business; a couple of veterinary nurses, another vet, an office manager who was retiring in a month, and Sandy.

Of all of them, she was the one who knew all the clients by name, humans included, and exactly how to make the old, grumpy computer system work. Once he'd discovered this, Michael had immediately given Sandy a pay rise.

'All good, all good. Ship shape, as it were.' She wasn't the tallest of women, but what she lacked in height she made up for in energy. 'The morning rush has been smooth so far.'

'That's good.' Michael moved behind Sandy and the reception desk to take off his coat. She turned in her chair to watch him.

'Everything's been on time and everyone's been in good health. One of those good mornings.'

'Long may it continue,' Michael murmured, smiling at her before disappearing from sight to refill his coffee mug.

'One of those tricky ones, isn't it,' said Sandy, standing to follow him. 'Obviously we want everyone to be fit and well, but we'd also quite like to have jobs.'

Michael chuckled.

'We can run a business doing regular check-ups.'

'Can we?' Sandy shrugged. 'Mrs Maisel is coming in later with Rat the pug.'

'Not Pug the rat,' said Michael.

Sandy grinned.

'Oh, how I wish there was a rat called Pug. Maybe I'll get one. I always did quite like rats.'

Michael watched her over the rim of his mug as

20

he tested his coffee.

'And who's my first appointment?' he asked when it became evident she'd become lost in thoughts about pet rats.

'Oh, a Mrs Taylor,' said Sandy, returning to her desk to check her computer screen. 'With a cocker spaniel called Lily. Just a check-up. They're new to the area, moved in last week. Guess where they moved into.' Sandy raised both eyebrows and pressed her lips together as she waited for Michael to catch up.

After a moment, Michael shrugged.

'Where?'

'The old farmhouse.' Sandy grinned, turning her back on him. 'Didn't you go view it when it was for sale?'

Michael, frozen, stared at the empty space Sandy had occupied as she moved back to her seat.

'Yes,' he said slowly. 'I did.' He blinked and looked up at her. 'And the new owners are coming in?'

'With their dog, Lily.'

'Oh.'

Sandy gave her boss a sideways look.

'She sounded very nice. An older lady. I asked where she'd moved from. They're English. Her, her husband and her grown-up daughter, so it's a family affair, which is nice.'

Michael's chest squeezed and he inhaled sharply.

'Yes. Nice.'

'Are you all right?'

Michael focused on Sandy's gaze and nodded.

'I'm fine. Thank you. What time are they coming in?'

Sandy checked the clock.

'Ten minutes.'

'Fine. Yes. Good. Thank you.' Michael walked away before Sandy could say anything else. He ventured into his office and left his coffee on his desk, then escaped into the staff toilets. Locking himself inside, he did what he needed to and then stared at his reflection in the little mirror over the sink.

He had gone to view that farmhouse, with its crumbling walls, spots of old damp and little two-bed cottage built weirdly next to it. The garden had been huge and out the back was a large paddock rented out to Bonnie McLeod and her daughter for their horses. Despite all the work the house had needed, it had come with the liveable cottage and a source of income. He could have filled the main house with cats and dogs and rented out the cottage once the work had been done. Or his mother could have moved there.

But his mother would never agree to leave Edinburgh, and all the cats and dogs in the world wouldn't stop Michael feeling as if he was rattling around that large house by himself.

And then it had sold and the dream had vanished.

It wasn't this woman's fault that he hadn't put an

offer in. It just hadn't been meant to be; at least, that's what his mother had said.

He exhaled slowly, searching his reflected tired, dark eyes.

There would be other houses, there would be other opportunities. Maybe next time he would be brave enough to go it alone. Or maybe, just maybe, he'd meet someone before that opportunity arose.

For now, though, there was a new dog to meet.

Michael attempted a smile, took another steadying breath, and went out to the consultation room to prepare.

The computer alerted him that Lily and her owner had arrived, so once he was sure the table was clean, he opened the door and called Lily's name. A toffee-coloured cocker spaniel bounced up as the woman holding her lead stood. Lily came right up to the door and then stopped, digging in her claws.

'Oh, come on, Lil,' said the woman holding the lead.

Michael smiled at the dog and fetched some biscuits from the tin by his computer. Sitting on the floor inside the consultation room, Michael held out an open hand with a biscuit laid on his palm.

'Hello, Lily,' he said gently. 'Nothing to be scared of. Do you want this biscuit? It's yummy, so I'm told. But you'll have to come here. It's not scary, I promise.'

Lily glanced up at the woman with her and then

sniffed the air as Michael talked. Eventually, slowly, she took a few steps forward and reached her nose towards the biscuit. Michael waited patiently.

'See? It's not scary. Everything's going to be okay. We're very friendly.'

Lily stepped inside the consultation room and gently took the biscuit from Michael's hand. He stroked her head and found his feet, looking up to the woman Lily had come in with.

'Good morning,' he said before his eyes met hers. He faltered and quickly turned away to take respite at his computer.

'Good morning,' she said in a soft English accent.

Mouth dry, Michael glanced up at the woman he had dreamed about that night and she smiled back.

Three

Frankie was still recovering from watching this man with a soft Edinburgh accent sit on the floor to entice her parents' dog over. Her cheeks and neck burned as a thick silence fell over the room, broken only by Lily who had discovered a taste for those biscuits on offer. She rushed over to the vet's side and sat, tail swishing across the floor.

'Oh, you want to be friends now?' he murmured to her, reaching down and ruffling her ears. Lily licked his hand and then pointedly sat back down.

'Well, let's see.' He glanced at his computer screen. 'You're new to the area?' he asked without looking at Frankie.

'Yeah. She's my parents' dog but something came up and they couldn't bring her, so I offered. We're using it as an excuse to explore the high street, aren't we, Lil?'

Lily ignored Frankie; she didn't have biscuits.

The vet smiled down at the dog.

'There's a nice park over the road, if you follow

the footpath between the buildings. There's a stream and grass, some benches. She'll love it.' Finally, he glanced up and caught Frankie's eye.

Her heart squeezed. Yes, she decided, he was definitely attractive, although not in a conventional way. But then, Frankie had long grown tired of conventional men. This one was tall, with a thin frame. He had short, dark hair and his face was a little long and worn; either too many days spent outside or too many late nights worked. His eyes were kind, although he wouldn't look at her long enough for her to figure out their colour. There was a chance they were only kind because he was putting all of his attention on Lily, but as vets went, that was what Frankie was after.

'A check-up and booster shots, yes?'

Frankie nodded.

'And how is she settling in?' he asked, taking another biscuit and lowering himself to Lily's level.

'Good. She's excited about having so much space to run around in. The garden is about three times the size of what she's used to. She hasn't quite gotten around to sniffing everything yet. She was a little stressed on moving day and the day after, but nothing a lot of cuddles didn't fix.'

The vet smiled and pressed a stethoscope to Lily's chest, letting her nibble on the biscuit in his hand to keep her still. Frankie waited, aware that he was trying to listen.

'Anything you're concerned about?' he asked,

shifting his position to feel Lily over.

'Nope.'

Was it Frankie's imagination or did he just glance up at her?

He checked Lily's teeth and then gave her the last of the biscuit.

'She's in good health,' he declared, standing. 'She's five now?'

Frankie nodded.

'Her heart sounds good. You might want to give her teeth an extra clean, but other than that, she's seems to be doing well.'

'Oh, good. Thank you.'

The vet turned to prepare the injections and Lily waited patiently, sitting beside him, her tail swishing across the floor. Frankie watched silently. He turned, gave Lily another biscuit and quickly pinched her scruff and injected the vaccine.

'Brave girl,' he murmured, rubbing the injection site better.

Lily shook herself and wandered over to Frankie for a reassuring stroke of the head. The vet returned to typing away at his keyboard. Lily trotted back to him and sat, just in case he magically produced another biscuit.

'How long have you had her?' he asked, peering down at Lily and smiling.

Frankie caught herself staring at that smile.

'Oh, erm, since she was a puppy. My parents brought her home at eight weeks old. Although I didn't see her much then.'

'Oh?'

'No, I was away a lot for work. It's only in the last year that I've been around and part of her life. I think that's why I offered to bring her today. I feel like we need to bond more.'

The vet looked her in the eye and something inside Frankie shifted.

'When was she last treated for fleas and worms?' he asked.

Frankie hesitated, still thinking about his smile. She snapped out of it and blustered a little.

'Erm, oh, I don't know. Erm, I can find out?'

The vet nodded, brushing down his hands.

'Yes. Feel free to call or pop in any time to discuss what you might need. But make sure she's up to date. There's a lot of tics around these parts, do you know how to remove tics?'

Frankie blinked.

'No. But I hear they're tricky.' Unable to stop herself, she added under her breath, 'They're tic-ky.'

Appearing to have not heard her, the vet nodded, avoiding her gaze.

'They are. If you spot one, don't touch it. Give us a call and bring her in. We can remove it and give you a lesson on how to do it.'

Frankie nodded.

'Great, thank you.'

'And I always recommend bringing her in whenever you're walking past, for a cuddle and a treat. So she doesn't associate us with needles and scary things. Sandy is always up for a cuddle with a cute dog.' He ruffled Lily's ears and she gave him her paw. Smiling, the vet glanced up at Frankie and did a double take at her expression. 'Sandy. She's our head receptionist. You'll have met her when you came in?'

'Oh, yes. Thank you. I have to say, everyone's been so friendly around here.'

The vet smiled again and nodded, but turned away. Frankie's smile dropped. That hadn't quite been the reaction she'd been hoping for. Fidgeting as he typed something else on the computer's keyboard, she inadvertently checked for a wedding ring. Would a vet wear a wedding ring? Considering where their hands had to go...

Not that it mattered. He didn't seem that interested, and yet there was something about him. She couldn't quite take her eyes from him, and there was something in the air. Although that might have been Lily.

He turned on her, breaking her thoughts.

'All done. Bye, Lily. Stay out of trouble.' He gave the dog a quick ruffle and then smiled at Frankie. Her breath caught, but she managed to nod and, picking up Lily's lead, herded the dog out and back into the waiting room. The door closed behind her.

Taking a breath, Frankie wandered over to the reception desk where a blonde woman was making kissy faces at Lily. Tail wagging, the dog pulled on the end of her lead and jumped up at the desk, stretching as tall as she could.

The woman's name tag on her chest declared her to be Sandy, the head receptionist.

'How did that go? I would ask if you got any treats, but Michael always has treats on him,' Sandy told Lily. She grinned up at Frankie. 'Just gotta wait until he's finished writing up your notes.'

'Of course, no problem.'

'So, you're new to the area. Bought the old farm-house on the edge of town? Very brave of you.'

Frankie barked a laugh.

'Yeah, it is a bit of a mess. But I was after a project.'

'Hmm.' Sandy's eyes narrowed as she took Frankie in, and Frankie's insides stilled. She stiffened, desperately trying to relax and breathe. 'It must be full of workmen,' Sandy continued.

'Not quite yet. I'm hoping to do a lot of the work myself, but there will be builders and I'll be getting an electrician and plumber in. There's no way I'm doing any of that!'

Sandy grinned.

'Bit of a property developer, are you?'

Frankie shrugged.

'I'm looking for a career change. I recently sold my house in London – boy, that was a wreck. I'd just left a big, erm, project and was bored, so started trying some of the work myself, thanks to videos online. And it was more fun than I thought, so when the farmhouse came up...' Frankie drifted off, wondering how much to divulge. 'I've always wanted to move to Scotland but was too scared. I don't know anyone up here, so I thought I'd wait to find a man or if I could convince a friend to move with me. And then I just thought, sod it! I can do this on my own. So, I dragged my parents up instead.'

They laughed.

'Lily's their dog, although I'm hoping to get my own once the house is in a better state.'

'How exciting! A little brother or sister,' Sandy told Lily. Then she stopped. 'No, a little niece or nephew?'

Sandy and Frankie stared at one another, both trying to work it out.

'Yeah, a little nephew, I think,' said Frankie slowly.

'Well, if you ever want to take a break, the pub over the road does a mean lunch or evening drinks. It's quiz night on Thursday, if you want to join my team?'

Frankie's eyes widened, her heart pounding.

'Oh, yes. That would be...wonderful. Yes. I'm Frankie, by the way.'

Sandy chuckled and pulled out a pen and paper.

'Lovely to meet you, Frankie. I'm Sandy. Here. This is my number. Give me a shout whenever you're free.'

'Honestly? I'm free whenever,' said Frankie, taking the piece of paper.

'Oh, Michael's done.' Sandy told her the amount to be paid and Frankie flashed her phone over the card reader. 'Well, I get a long lunch on Wednesdays, if you're up for the pub?'

Frankie nodded.

'I'm always up for a pub lunch.'

Sandy laughed.

'Oh, I think we might get on! Great. Meet you outside here on Wednesday, at twelve?'

'Fantastic. Thank you. See you then.'

'See you then. Bye, Lily!'

Frankie walked out of the vets with a grin plastered on her face, glancing at the footpath over the road that led between two buildings and presumably to a park. Smiling up at the decorations unlit in the grey afternoon light, she crossed the road with Lily and they went to explore.

'Mum! Dad! We're back. And if Lily ever needs to go back to the vets, I can take her!'

Lily ran full speed through the cottage after Frankie unclipped her lead. She led Frankie into the kitchen where her parents sat at the table. She frowned at them.

'I thought you were both too busy to take Lily?'

'We are!' proclaimed her father, holding up muddy hands. 'I've marked out where I want my garden and made a start on clearing things. Hope you don't mind.'

'Of course not,' said Frankie, taking a seat.

'And my yoga class was a bit dismal,' her mother told her. 'It smelled of feet. And everyone was a bit quiet. No one wanted a chat before or after. How did it go?'

'Great. I'm meeting Sandy, she's the receptionist, for lunch on Wednesday, she seems very nice. Lily got a clean bill of health, and the vet is hot. So, you know, anytime she needs to go, I can take her. He suggested popping in with Lily now and then so she can make friends with everyone.'

Her parents stared at her and then her father stood.

'Well, I'm glad Lil is okay. C'mon Lily, come help me dig.'

They watched as he led Lily out of the back door. Frankie turned to find her mother smiling at her.

'Hot, huh?'

Frankie shrugged.

'Gorgeous? Is that better? Hot's probably the wrong word. He's attractive. Lily was scared to go in, so he got on the floor and tempted her in with biscuits.'

Irene raised an eyebrow.

'Well, can't argue with that.'

'I think his name's Michael. You know, in case

we ever need to ask for him. For Lily.'

'Yes, just in case. For Lily,' said Irene. 'Is he Scottish? Does he have an accent?'

'Uh-huh. One of those soft, Edinburgh accents,' said Frankie.

Both women went off into their own worlds for a moment.

'Is he married?' Irene asked dreamily.

'I have no idea. It didn't come up.'

'Did he flirt with you?'

Frankie laughed.

'Nope. Not even a little bit. I've probably got more chance with Sandy. She asked about the house.'

'How did she know about the house?'

'Mum, she has our address.'

'Oh, of course. Right.' Irene fidgeted. 'You will be careful, won't you.'

'Yes, Mum. It's okay. Been there, done that. It'll all be fine.'

Irene nodded.

'Good, okay.'

'So, you're not going back to yoga?'

'I don't know.' Irene sniffed and pulled a face. 'I'm not sure it's for me. I've never wanted to fart so much in a quiet room filled with people before. Plus, you know, it hurt. Load of spiritual nonsense, too. No. So, I came home, had a cup of tea and look what I found.' She turned her tablet round so Frankie could see the screen.

'Photography?'

'Hmm. A photography course. Oh, and painting classes. They could be fun. The thing is...' Irene trailed off and looked up at her daughter.

'What's the thing?'

'They're in Edinburgh.'

Frankie grinned.

'Want me to come with you?'

Irene nodded.

'Not necessarily to the classes. I can't make friends if you're cramping my style,' she said with a smile. 'But, you said you wanted day trips into the city. Maybe we could go there and back together?'

Frankie nodded.

'Of course! I'd love to.'

'And you know what I'd really love to find?'

'What's that, Mum?'

'A book club.'

Four

Michael threw his keys into their bowl with a clatter and made his way to the bedroom. On autopilot, he stripped his clothes and padded into the shower, languishing under the heat while his stomach growled. It had been another one of those days where he'd stopped on the high street and considered buying a place in Bekburn. The day hadn't been overly long, but only because he'd designed it that way. It would have been nice to have spent the early evening winding down, helping to shut up the practice before walking home, breathing in the cold, crisp air, looking out over the hills and maybe inviting some colleagues to the pub for a drink. Instead of having to get in his car early, attempt to miss the rush hour traffic, fail miserably and end up popping into his city practice to check on everything. Paperwork and phone calls completed, he'd managed to get through his front door at eight o'clock.

Now, hair damp and body refreshed, he fed Agnes and checked the cupboards.

'Looks like there's only food for you,' he told her as she licked the last of the meal from her bowl and then rubbed herself against his legs. He crouched to stroke her, rubbing her ears as he considered a takeaway. He'd need to go shopping at some point. When would he fit that in? Unless he went now.

Sighing, Michael checked the time and pulled a face. Grabbing his phone, he called the local Indian restaurant and placed a delivery order. They knew him, knew his regular order, so it took no time at all. Turning on the Christmas lights adorning the little plastic tree in the corner, Michael then poured a glass of wine and allowed himself a moment to relax, sitting back on his sofa. Agnes jumped up and walked over his lap to get to the other side, where she sat, staring out of the window into the Edinburgh night. Michael sipped his wine, watching her. He jumped as his doorbell rang. Answering via video, Michael told the delivery driver he'd be right there and then he wandered down to collect his food and have a quick chat.

Dishing up his order onto a plate and topping up his wine, Michael settled back on the sofa and flicked the TV on. Agnes came to investigate what was on offer and got a small piece of poppadom for her troubles before she was scooped up and placed on the floor.

'This is mine. Go away,' Michael told her.

Agnes glared up at him and then sauntered away, back to the window.

There was nothing on TV but Michael left it on while he ate. Once finished, he tidied the hardly touched kitchen, stacking his dishwasher, and then made himself a cup of tea. While the kettle boiled, he turned on his laptop at his little makeshift desk on a small dining table that was never used for dining.

Sitting down with his cup of tea, Michael checked his emails and then glanced at his phone. It stared back. Picking it up, he took it over to the window and stood beside Agnes, trying to work out what she was watching as he listened to his phone ringing.

'Hello?'

'Hi, Mum. It's me.'

'I know, your name comes up.'

'Okay.' Michael sighed through his nose. 'You said hello as if you didn't know who it was.'

'Just in case it wasn't you.'

Michael stroked Agnes's head and the cat leaned into him.

'Who else would it be?'

'I don't know. A policeman calling to tell me you've been in a horrific car accident, or a burglar who's broken in and beaten you round the head.'

There was a pause as Michael considered this.

'I don't think they'd call you using my phone,' he said.

'How else would they get my number?'

'Fair point. And why is the burglar calling you?'

'To tell me I'm next. Or maybe because he's filled with remorse at what he's done and he wants forgiveness.'

'Would you forgive him?'

'Of course not! I'd be straight down there to give him as good as he gave!'

Michael laughed.

'I don't doubt it,' he told her.

'Are you all right? Why are you calling so late?'

'I'm fine, Mum. I was about to do some work—'

'No! You shouldn't be working at this hour. Your father—'

'I know, I know. Dad used to work all the evenings, but you were only angry because you missed him. I don't have a wife to miss me, Mum. Or kids I should be spending time with. Just Agnes, and she doesn't mind me working as long as she gets fed.'

Esme sighed down the phone.

'I just worry about you.'

'Evidently,' said Michael, smiling. 'Anyway, I'm not working. I'm talking to you.' He sat on the sofa, stroking Agnes who stayed looking out of the window. 'Do you remember that farmhouse I went to view? In Bekburn?'

'Sort of.'

'I met the new owner today.'

'Oh?'

'She brought her parents' dog in for a check-up. Cocker spaniel, very sweet.'

'Her parents' dog? How old was she?'

'Five, I think.'

'The woman, not the dog!'

'Oh. I don't know. Thirties, probably.'

'Late? Early?'

'Does it matter?'

Esme huffed down the phone and Michael frowned.

'She's just bought a huge house, Mum. She's probably married. Moved in with her husband and their kids. Why else would someone buy such a large house?'

'Fine. I suppose. Did you ask if she was married?'

'It's not really something you can bring up. Hi, yes, your dog's heart sounds fine but are you single?'

Esme chuckled.

'No, I suppose not. There's a way to bring it up, though. There's always a way.'

'Mum,' Michael started after another pause, 'did I make a mistake not buying that farmhouse?'

Esme sighed.

'You wanted me to move down there with you, remember? I'm not leaving Edinburgh, Michael. You would have moved there by yourself. You wouldn't have been happy. And think of the commute! Most of your work is here. Unless you're thinking of cutting back?' There was a glimmer of hope in his mother's voice.

Michael shrugged the question off.

'You're right. I wouldn't have been happy,' he

said.

'How is work?' Esme asked after another slight pause.

'Good. Today was good. I just need to finish preparing for tomorrow before bed. I'm spending the morning and maybe early afternoon on the streets before going into the practice. I checked in with the practice on my way home today, I didn't miss much, thankfully.'

'Okay. Don't work too hard, all right?'

Michael promised his mother he wouldn't.

'What about you? What have you been up to?'

'Oh, well, there's been all the gossip. Ballroom dancing and everything.'

'Oh?' Michael grinned.

'Yes. I'll tell you all about it when we meet for cake. Are we still doing that?'

'Of course. I wouldn't miss it.'

'Wonderful.'

They finished the conversation, wishing each other a good night, and finally, Michael sat at his laptop and began preparing the paperwork needed for the next day.

Michael was often told by visiting relatives, friends and the odd girlfriend what a magical city he lived in. It wasn't that he didn't appreciate it, with its worn stone buildings and deep history, it was that he got to see some of the reality behind the tourist cloak. Michael was used to the grandeur and the architecture and the castle up on its hill, but what he would never get used to was how much money was spent in this great, magical city and yet how many of its residents lived on the streets. It wasn't something he'd noticed much when he was growing up. He'd been too preoccupied with what could be, what career path he would follow, where he would travel, when he might fall madly in love, that he didn't see much of what was around him. As that worked itself out – the girlfriends coming and going, the gap year spent travelling that only made him sick, and then following in his father's career footsteps and being handed the family business – he started to notice the parts of Edinburgh that they didn't want the tourists to see.

It started with a man who had frequented the corner of Michael's street. Michael walked past him every morning and evening until he could no longer ignore how rude he was being in not stopping to ask the man how he was. His name had been Greg and he'd been quiet and friendly, living on the streets as a last resort after he lost his job and couldn't afford the rent. Michael had brought Greg a home-brewed coffee every morning and a sandwich every evening. Then, one afternoon, a note was put through Michael's door and Greg was gone. To live with a cousin in London, thanks for the kindness, take care of yourself.

That experience had played on Michael's mind until a few months later when he'd met Sharon, forced onto the streets after her marriage turned nasty, and she'd taken her dog with her. Michael had started a conversation almost immediately, giving Sharon's old Staffie cuddles until she let slip that she was worried about the dog. Michael had looked up at her, his brain screaming at him until he told her that he was a vet and had a practice down the road.

'Come in on a Monday, Thursday or Friday, ask for me at reception and I'll see what I can do. Free of charge.'

The next day, Sharon had found the veterinary practice Michael's father had founded, asked for Michael by name and he'd given her a free consultation. Her dog was fine, it turned out, he just needed worming. Sharon was so overwhelmed, she'd been leaving with tears in her eyes when Michael had run after her with a handful of business cards.

'Give these to anyone living rough with pets. Let them know any time they're worried, they can come in and see me.'

That was how Michael had come to know the local homeless community of Edinburgh and how, one day, a woman named Claire had tracked him down. She was in the process of starting up a charity doing exactly what he was doing but out on the streets, taking the veterinary care to the pets wherever they were needed across the city.

'We need a head vet,' she'd told him.

He hadn't even needed to consider it.

Five

'I'll meet you back here. Have fun!' Frankie waved her mother off as Irene disappeared into the building for her first photography class. They'd be walking around Princes Street Gardens once the class was underway, so Frankie walked in the opposite direction. She knew the Old Town by heart, anyway. It would do her good to learn the streets of New Town. There was a lot on offer this side of Princes Street Gardens. Frankie considered wandering through Stockbridge to the botanical gardens, or perhaps to Dean's Village to see if she could spot any social media influencers taking advantage of the beautiful buildings by the Water of Leith.

She paused by the private gardens alongside Queen Street and checked the distances on her phone. They were both fairly close, so the botanical gardens it was; at least there was cake and a place to sit there. Unable to keep the smile from her lips, Frankie ambled down the road, trying to stay aware of her surroundings while staring up at the buildings. They were tall on either side, with black railings leading down below the road to the basement levels, and white-squared windows giving each building a sense of height. Most of them had five – Frankie counted – floors, but some had six. Were they houses? Or flats? Some were businesses and Frankie peered into the windows of each. She paused when she reached the sign off to the left for Circus Lane, the ever-popular site of so many Instagrammers. Checking her map, Frankie ducked into the lane where the road became less tarmac and more paved. She'd hardly call it cobbled. Trees sprung up on her right, offering a splash of cool green against the cream and grey stone. Garages gave way to mews and beautiful plants climbing up walls. Frankie shook her head, grinning. It was pretty, she had to admit, but she wasn't convinced it deserved the hype. Still, she slowed her pace, enjoying the calm, despite being so close to the city centre.

Out the other side, she turned right and headed towards Stockbridge Market. She was hardly discovering new places; she'd walked this way often on previous visits, but the comfort of the familiar was good. Edinburgh had always felt like home, from the moment she'd stepped foot inside the city. Although, the first time she'd entered the city had been on a bus. On the top of a double decker as it drove through West End, rounded a corner and there, much to Frankie's delight, had been a castle on top of a hill. She hadn't really believed people when they'd told her of the magic of Edinburgh, but she felt it the moment she saw the castle. Unable to take her eyes from it as the bus passed, Frankie still had trouble not staring at it whenever it was in view. Would she ever not look like a tourist?

She didn't look like a tourist now, she thought, pushing her phone into her pocket. She was striding purposefully through Stockbridge, knowing exactly where she was headed, and home was only a tram ride and a forty-five-minute drive away.

Grinning, Frankie stopped herself from skipping.

She nearly missed her right turning, having to back track a little and take on the tourist costume again while she checked the map on her phone. Heading down a residential road lined with green trees, pretty gardens and cream-grey two-storey houses with an excess of chimneys, her memory began to fill in the blanks. She couldn't help but go on tiptoe to check over walls and look at particular houses. How much would they cost? Had she made a mistake buying in the countryside? A house in the city would have been exciting.

With a guilty pang, Frankie remembered the number in her bank accounts and swallowed hard. She could afford to buy a house in the city as well as the countryside if she wanted to. And why shouldn't she? She'd worked hard for that money.

Her stomach turned. Shaking her head, Frankie

marched on, turning left as a brown tourist sign pointed the way to the botanical gardens. On her right was a streamside walk and, for a moment, Frankie considered finding a gate to reach the path. Instead, she continued, looking up at the old tenement houses on the other side of the stream. Ahead, the path veered to the right to cut the corner away from the road, and Frankie went to follow it eagerly, only hesitating when she spotted a group of people at the bench.

Two men, a woman and a little terrier. The dog was wagging its tail while one of the men crouched and examined its eyes.

Frankie's gaze found the words on the back of the woman's jacket; Vets On Streets. Her heart squeezed and she found herself smiling down at the dog. How strange, she thought, to bump into the very charity she had supported all these years, hard at work. The woman was talking with the dog's evident owner, a man who, judging by his possessions, was sleeping rough. Frankie thought back to her bank account and shuddered.

Then she hesitated, her step faltering, as the man examining the dog glanced up and caught her eye.

For a moment, the world around them froze. His eyes widened ever so slightly. She wouldn't have noticed if she hadn't been staring right at them, holding her breath, wondering if she should do something. Say something.

In the end, she attempted a smile which probably came across as a quick grimace, and walked past Michael the vet, crouching in front of the little terrier. Heart pounding, she slowed her pace a little, not daring to glance back. When she got to a point where she was about to round a corner and disappear from view, she risked it, looking over her shoulder.

Michael was standing, talking and smiling with the woman, but then he glanced over and caught Frankie's eye once again. Turning back so fast that she almost tripped, Frankie stormed on towards the botanical gardens.

Once inside, she headed for the café by the house overlooking the city. The gardens were filled with the Christmas light display that turned on when darkness fell, but they were all off now. The café itself was strewn with tasteful Christmas decorations, plant-themed baubles hanging out of the way, a little tinsel on the cake display case and fairy lights around the large windows. She bought herself a coffee and a slice of cake, and managed to get a table by the window. Sipping her coffee, looking out at the grey December day, something inside Frankie twisted. Not only was her parents' vet incredibly attractive, he worked for a charity she'd discovered on social media and had been donating to monthly ever since. What were the odds? It flashed through Frankie's mind that she could get directly involved with the charity now that she didn't have a job but did have zeros burning holes in her bank accounts. She slid a forkful of cake into her mouth, eyes glazing as she thought it through. It might solve some of her guilt and it would certainly give her a purpose, it would help people, and maybe it would mean she could spend time with Michael.

Six

That morning had started as any other for Michael. He walked through the city with his travel mug of coffee having woken his neighbours with light piano music after feeding Agnes her breakfast. Michael's breakfast was his coffee. He walked quickly, although he didn't mean to. His long legs stretching out before him as he lost himself in thoughts of his dream that night. He'd dreamed of her again, of the dark-haired woman in his bed, her lips on his, and as she'd kissed him, straddling him, her hair falling down her bare back, he'd calmly noted that she was the woman from the Bekburn practice, the new owner of the farmhouse. How had he dreamed about her so clearly before meeting her? There had to be an explanation. Had he walked past her in the city? Maybe he'd seen her in Bekburn, wandering past the veterinary practice window.

'Beautiful morning, isn't it,' he said to the veterinary nurse waiting for him at the corner of the road. She smiled, lugging her bag over her shoulder.

'Bit chilly,' Lucia said in her smooth Italian accent.

Michael shrugged, looking up at the solid grey sky.

'It's warmer than it could be. How was your weekend?'

'Good. We tried that restaurant you recommended. It was lovely.'

'Oh, good.'

'How was yours?'

'Busy. I spent it working.'

Lucia rolled her eyes.

'Of course you did. And you haven't stopped all week, have you? Why? Don't you know how to relax?'

Michael smiled, trying to take the comment with good nature, but still, it stung a little.

'Of course. I like working. I caught up on some admin, saw some clients who couldn't make it during the week. Don't worry, I relaxed as well.' Although not much, he admitted to himself. Of course he worked all weekend, what else was he supposed to do?

'You should get a hobby,' said Lucia, as if reading his mind.

Michael ignored that.

'Where to first?'

Lucia checked a list on her phone.

'Danny and Diesel.'

Michael smiled.

'Great. Did we get the toys for Diesel? We promised him toys last time.'

Lucia patted the bag.

'We might even have time for a play.'

They made their way to meet Danny, chatting as they went, about the weather, about Lucia's week-end, about what the rest of the morning entailed.

By eleven o'clock, they'd seen three dogs and two cats, and were meeting with their last patient of the day. Michael would then grab some lunch from a sandwich shop he'd spotted and make his way to the city practice for the remainder of his day's consultations. While he was still happy to see the pets of the homeless community in his practice, he did enjoy the morning city air on days like this. Edgar the terrier barked a greeting as Michael and Lucia approached and Edgar's human, a young man named Robbie, stood up and dusted himself down. Robbie moved around quite a bit, but they'd agreed to meet regularly at this spot by the stream, where there was space away from the road and a bench for Robbie to rest on. They exchanged pleasantries as Edgar covered Lucia with licks, tail wagging furiously, and then Robbie mentioned that the dog had developed a lump on his belly.

'Well, let's take a look, shall we?' Michael crouched and gave Edgar a cuddle, ruffling his ears and slipping the dog a treat that Lucia had passed over. As Edgar relaxed a little, Michael found the small lump Robbie was concerned about and did an examination. Edgar allowed it, whining a little at being made to stay still. Michael did a quick check of the dog's ears and teeth while he had him.

'It shouldn't be anything to worry about. It seems like a fatty lump. But if you notice it getting bigger or changing, or if Edgar's behaviour changes at all, then either let us know next time we're around or come see me at my practice. You know the address?'

Robbie nodded.

'Thanks, Michael. Really appreciate it.'

'Of course. Anything for a cute face.' Michael blew Edgar a kiss and the dog tried to lick him back.

'He only says that to the dogs,' Lucia remarked as Michael stepped aside so she could flea and worm Edgar.

Michael laughed, standing, his back complaining along with his knees. He refused to listen to his joints, he absolutely was not getting too old for this, no matter what they said. He glanced up at the light grey sky, his neck clicking as he stretched his back. Lucia was chatting to Robbie, so Michael took a moment to look around the road. It was quiet, with a school over the wall and houses on the other side of the stream. The odd car or van drove past and there were a few people wandering down the path. An elderly man with a walking stick and a bag of shopping. A woman with a baby wrapped to her chest, strolling along, looking up at the trees and talking gently to her child. She studied Michael, Lucia and Robbie for a moment, a blank expression in her eyes, until she caught sight of Edgar. She smiled and Michael smiled back, but she ignored him. He lifted his eyebrows. Some people only ever saw the animals. Which, considering he was a vet, was probably what Michael should have been doing, but for some reason he'd always seen the people with the animals. His father had once called him a rare breed and told him to nurture that particular skill. He'd taught Michael a lot of important lessons. Michael sighed, wondering, not for the first time, what his father would have made of this business decision to give away free veterinary care. His mother claimed he would have loved it and secretly been annoyed he hadn't thought of it. But then, his father was one of those people who only saw the animals and not the people.

Lucia moved away and Michael crouched to give Edgar more affection. While cuddling the dog, he checked his eyes. Was one a little red? No, on closer inspection, it was fine and Edgar licked the air between them. Michael ruffled his ears and then glanced up for no reason.

He stopped, his mind falling silent as he caught the eye of the woman walking towards them. Her gaze lingered on Robbie and Lucia, and then landed on him for a moment. As she passed, she gave a quick, warm smile. Michael's chest tightened.

The dreams came flooding back. The one from last night and from the beginning of the week. He knew those eyes, those lips, that long dark hair. He'd kissed that skin, he'd breathed her in.

It had to be a coincidence. The city was full of people, probably a good half of them women, and many were beautiful. Some were chest-tighteningly beautiful. This one didn't live in the city, though, she lived in the farmhouse he'd wanted in Bekburn.

That had to be it. It wasn't that she was beautiful, or that he'd dreamed of kissing her. It was the house. She represented what he'd lost, a symbol of regret. That had to be it.

Michael caught himself watching her pass, although she was looking elsewhere. He forced himself to look away, to attempt to work out what Robbie and Lucia were discussing. To do his job. But he couldn't help seeking the woman out again. She paused just as the road curved, and looked back. Their eyes met and, even from this distance, his mind screamed at him to look away, but he couldn't. She turned quickly and hurried out of sight.

Heart pounding far more than it should have been, Michael blinked and turned back to his patient. Lucia and Robbie were waiting for him.

'Remember, any worries, come see me,' he told Robbie, snapping out of it and shaking the man's hand before they left them to their day.

'Are you all right?' Lucia asked.

'Of course.'

'Did you know that woman?'

'She's just moved to Bekburn. Brought her dog into my practice,' he explained. It was almost the full truth.

'Small world,' Lucia murmured as they wandered away from Robbie and Edgar. 'Another morning well spent. What are you doing for lunch?'

'I was going to grab a sandwich. You?'

'I'm meeting a friend, so home first to wash up. See you next week?'

'Absolutely. Have a good one.'

They parted ways and Michael found the sandwich shop he'd spotted. After a short wait, he bought a sandwich and a coffee, and took a leisurely stroll to his city practice where an afternoon of patients and consultations awaited. He didn't have time to revisit his dreams again but as he walked to his practice, he considered the reality that the woman represented what could have been and nothing more.

'What are you getting Mum for Christmas?'

'I'm good, thank you, Jamie,' said Michael as he wiped down the consulting table for the final time that day. It had been a long day, starting at seven and finishing at seven. His legs ached with exhaustion and his back was stiffening. It was becoming hard to concentrate on anything other than the idea of a hot shower and something delicious to eat.

'Sorry. How are you?' asked Jamie, enunciating as he spoke.

'I'm all right. How are you?'

'All right? A moment ago you were good.'

'Things change.'

Jamie sighed down the phone.

'Is this my fault?'

'What? No. Of course not.' Michael left a pause, and then asked, 'What time is it there?' He grinned as he asked, almost feeling his brother rolling his eyes all the way in Australia.

'It's five in the morning.'

'Why on earth are you up at five in the morning?' Michael asked, switching off the computer.

'To call you.'

'You couldn't have waited an hour? It's only seven in the evening here.'

'I know. And you say "only seven", but where are you, Mike?'

Michael had the decency to hesitate.

'At Dad's practice.'

'Okay, first of all, it's your practice. Secondly, it's seven in the evening. Go home!'

'I am doing! Someone called me and is making me shut up the practice slower than usual.'

'I knew it. I knew this would be my fault.'

'Oh, you're just cranky from lack of sleep.' Michael grinned, hearing his big brother stifle a laugh.

'So, pleasantries done with – and by the way, it's too early here for pleasantries, but I'll forgive you – what are you getting Mum for Christmas?'

Michael shrugged to himself, almost dislodging the phone from where it was nestled between his ear and shoulder as he turned off the light and closed the door on the consultation room.

'I don't know.'

'Has she mentioned anything she'd like?'

'Some books, maybe. For her book club.'

'I can send her some books.'

'Her umbrella broke last week.'

'I can send her an umbrella.'

'Most of all, I think she misses you and her grandchildren.'

'Ah... Yes, I'm working on that.'

'Do you need me to send you money?' Michael asked.

Jamie sighed.

'No. We're getting there. It's just slow going. Things are a bit tight right now.'

'Maybe things would be cheaper if you moved back to Scotland? There's not a Christmas present I could give Mum that would top that,' said Michael, making his way to his office to pick up his coat and laptop bag. He nodded to two nurses on their way out.

'Tempting, but I don't remember the last time I broke an umbrella,' said Jamie. 'Anyway, what's up with you? Why are you only all right?'

'Oh, it's nothing. It's... It's nothing. Remember that farmhouse in Bekburn I viewed?'

'No.'

'Well, I met the new owner this week. And then I saw her again this morning.'

'You like her? That's one way of getting a rural house.'

Michael pulled a face.

'I dreamt about her.'

'Wow. She's gotten under your skin that much? Just how gorgeous is she?'

Michael ignored that question.

'It's just because of the house, though,' he told Jamie as much as himself. 'Maybe I should have made an offer on it. Maybe I should be looking at a little country idle somewhere out there. Maybe it's time to leave the city.'

Jamie tutted.

'Or maybe you saw a pretty face. Maybe this is about the girl and not about the house. Think about it, Michael. How did you feel when you saw that house had sold?'

Michael gave this some consideration.

'A little deflated. But maybe a little relieved, too. It needs so much work. I never would have managed it. Plus, what would I want a house that big for when there's just me.'

'There!' shouted Jamie, making Michael jump. 'Right there! This isn't about the house, Michael. Is this woman single? Next time you see her, ask her out.'

'It's not as simple as—'

'I dare you,' said Jamie.

Smiling, Michael shook his head.

'I have to go lock up the practice now,' he told his brother. 'Go have some breakfast or something.'

'Had it. I'm off to the gym before work.'

'Fine. Love to the family.'

'Remember, Mikey, I dared you. No! I double dare you. Now you have to do it.'

'All right, all right. Goodbye.'

Michael hung up the phone and then stared at the blank screen, smiling to himself. His brother's words repeated in his mind as his smile faded and an image of the dark-haired woman who owned the farmhouse formed in front of him.

If only it were that easy.

Seven

Frankie had decided to start downstairs, in the kitchen. The best thing to do, she figured, was to rip everything out, strip it all back and start again, safe in the knowledge that her parents had a working kitchen only a short walk across the driveway. Destroying the old kitchen was easy enough. She'd removed all the cupboard doors carefully and put them to one side, wondering if they'd be useful for something else one day. Maybe she'd have a large garage built on the other side of the driveway, opposite the cottage, and these doors could be used for cupboard storage. Or she could give them away to someone more crafty and talented than herself.

She attempted to remove the rest of the cupboards in the same fashion, aware that someone could find a use for them, but the wood splintered and she realised she'd have to make a note of what piece of wood went with the other pieces, and soon she was yanking and smashing the remains of the kitchen apart.

Scotland was colder than London. It was a fact

she'd known for a long time, but for some reason she hadn't fully acknowledged it before. The back door needed replacing, but for now a chilled December wind blew through the cracks every now and then, blasting her. Shivering after one particularly strong gust, Frankie swore at the wind and went to find her hat, scarf and a coat.

'Ridiculous,' she muttered, glancing at the radiator. She could put the heating on, but Frankie knew from experience that she'd have to open the back door soon to let out the dust, and despite all those zeroes in her bank accounts, she wasn't wasting money on lost heat. Those zeroes were precious and needed to be spent in the right way, for the right causes. Heating the kitchen while she worked was not worthy enough.

Within a couple of hours, the old kitchen was gone and her father appeared just as she was tidying up.

'You did demolition without me?' he asked, passing her a cup of coffee.

'You were asleep,' she pointed out.

'You could have waited.'

'Nope. Gotta keep busy, Dad.' Frankie grinned at her father. 'Anyway, you're just in time to help me shift this lot. Everything needs to go outside.'

'Do you think you might need a skip?' Geoff asked, surveying the mess.

'Yes. I ordered one this morning, it's coming in three days. We'll make a pile for now. Take care with those cupboard doors, they're in good nick.'

'For what?'

'Oh, I don't know. Someone might want them. Or maybe they could go in a brand new double garage?'

Geoff's eyes lit up.

'Double or triple?'

Frankie laughed.

'Let's sort the house out first.'

Her father picked up the first of the cupboard doors.

'If that's the case, these shouldn't go outside. Have you been out there? Blowing a gale.'

'I'm aware,' said Frankie, gesturing to the open back door and then the many layers and thick coat she was wearing. 'Come on, I've got the kitchen bloke coming in an hour. Let's see how much we can clear. Put those cupboard doors in the dining room next door for now.'

Forty-five minutes later, the kitchen was clear and Geoff had declared that he would attempt a dog walk down to the high street. If he wasn't back in an hour, they were to assume he'd been blown away and were to send an aerial search party. Irene, more concerned with the amount of trees around, accompanied him, having failed to talk him out of the walk until the wind had died down.

Alone on her property for the first time, Frankie drained her third cup of coffee that morning and surveyed the empty room that had once been the kitchen.

Her chest tightened at the sight, her breathing becoming short.

'Ah! No,' she told herself. 'Don't you dare. There's nothing to panic about.' She put down her cup and placed a hand on her chest, purposefully breathing deep. 'Everything's all right. Everything's going to be fine. This is going to be a wonderful adventure. You do not miss London. There's nothing to miss. This is going to be fun. You just have to get the horrible building bit out of the way first. Give it time.' She took another deep breath and moved to the window to stare out at the garden. In the distance, past the fence of the back garden boundary, two horses were peacefully grazing in a field that she, inexplicably, owned and rented to the horses' owners, and behind them were the hills.

It was beautiful. It was everything Frankie had dreamed about. And it was hers.

The smile was jolted off her face by a sharp knock at the front door.

The kitchen man had arrived, and he did bathrooms as well. She'd only spoken to his business partner on the phone. Curious as to his reaction at the amount of work that needed doing, Frankie answered the door and let him in. Her chest untightened and warmed at the sight of his face lighting up.

'Mrs Taylor? Gorgeous house,' he said, his gaze darting around the hallway, catching glimpses of the rooms beyond.

'Close enough. And thank you. It needs so much work, though. It'll need rewiring before any work starts, but I'd like to get the kitchen and bathroom installations booked in, if possible,' Frankie explained. 'Come on through. I've just finished ripping out the old kitchen.' He joined her in the newly empty room. 'And this wall is going to come down,' Frankie added, tapping her fist against the wall on her right.

'To create a big kitchen diner?'

'Yes, with a little orangery extension on the front of the dining room.'

He looked at her with surprise. Frankie gave a small shrug.

'While we're here, making a mess, I reckon we should make it the best we can.'

A smile bloomed on the man's face.

'And there are three bathrooms. One downstairs, a family one upstairs and a horrible en suite.'

The man laughed.

'I'm Frankie,' said Frankie, holding out her hand. He shook it, his fingers icy cold against the warmth of her recently gloved working hands.

'Iain,' he told her. 'What an incredible project. Right, so' – he pulled out a notebook and pen from his coat pocket – 'do you have ideas for how you want the kitchen laid out?'

Frankie grinned.

'Oh yes.'

Midday came around too fast. Frankie hadn't quite finished with Iain – they'd gotten lost in the details of kitchen materials and walk-in showers. He'd have to come back to go over the bathrooms, but that wasn't a problem. He was the third kitchen and bathroom installer she'd met with, and he was the first she'd managed to have a laugh with. He hadn't even minded when Lily had burst through upon returning from her morning walk. Iain was getting the contract, if he wanted it.

The bonus was that he hadn't seemed to recognise her.

Frankie wasn't recognised often, but every now and then she would hear another name that she knew she should respond to. As the years went by, it happened less and less. Part of the hope of moving to the rural Scottish Borders was that, eventually, it wouldn't happen at all.

Frankie jogged up the high street from the small car park and landed in front of Sandy, breathing hard, hands on her knees.

'Sorry I'm late,' she said between gasps of air. 'Kitchen man. Overran.'

When she straightened, Sandy was giving her a bemused smile.

'It's not a problem. I was about to go inside. It's getting a wee bit chilly.'

Frankie laughed.

'I imagine you Londoner types think it's freezing?' Sandy added, looking Frankie up and down.

'It's not as cold as I thought it would be,' Frankie said, thinking back to those blasts of cold air coming around the back door. 'Although that might be because I spent the morning ripping out a kitchen and then rushing here.'

There was a moment between them as Sandy's eyes widened and Frankie caught her breath, and then Sandy laughed and beckoned Frankie inside.

'Sounds like you need warmth and food.'

'Oh, yes please, definitely.'

Frankie followed Sandy inside and was immediately hit by the thick warmth of a cosy, traditional pub warmed by a roaring fire. There was even a golden Labrador asleep in front of the flames, although the dog opened one eye to watch them walk in. There were a few patrons, mostly older people sitting at tables eating lunch, and one young family with a toddler excited about the spoon of food coming towards them. Twinkling fairy lights gave the windows and bar a festive glow and tinsel had been hung around the period wooden beams.

'This is lovely,' Frankie breathed.

'Afternoon, Sandy,' said a woman from behind the bar. She spared a look at Frankie and then passed Sandy two menus.

'Hi, Poppy. This is Frankie. She's the one who

bought the big farmhouse.'

Poppy, her long brown hair gathered into a bun on the back of her head and her glasses pushed up her nose, gave Frankie another appraising look.

'Lovely to meet you,' said Frankie. 'This pub is amazing. I'll have to tell my parents about it, you'll probably end up seeing them every day.'

Poppy's face cracked as she smiled.

'Well, that would be lovely. We were a bit worried about some big business man or developer buying the farmhouse.'

'Oh, no. Just me and my parents. And we want to be a part of the community.'

'They're from London,' said Sandy, with a little too much meaning.

'Yeah, well, we moved here from London. Sort of. I moved here from London. My parents were living in Essex. But I've always wanted to live in Scotland. It's beautiful around here.'

Poppy looked Frankie up and down.

'Doing the farmhouse up, are you?'

'Yes. I did a renovation project back in London, but it was very small. Small but expensive, thanks to London prices. So now it's a big project with local tradespeople, and probably for the same money if I'm honest.' Frankie gave a nervous laugh.

'And you don't have family in Scotland?' Poppy asked.

'Oh. Erm, no.'

'I'll have a lemonade, please, Poppy,' Sandy said

quickly. 'Need to keep it light before the afternoon rush.'

'Of course, love. And for you?' Poppy glanced at Frankie.

'A lemonade would be great, thanks.'

Once they had their drinks, they found a table out of the way. All of the window tables were taken but Sandy positioned herself so she could just see outside.

'In case my boss shows up,' she said with a small laugh.

'Would he not like you being here? I don't want to get you in trouble,' said Frankie, getting comfortable and peering at the menu.

'Oh, no. He doesn't have a problem with a pub lunch. To be fair, he's a great boss. As long as the work gets done, he doesn't mind. But it means I really want to do a good job for him, you know? He's the best boss I've had. Nicer than the last practice owners. They were a bit...snappy.'

Frankie pulled a face.

'I think probably just a sandwich for me, but with chips. Do you want a side of chips?' Sandy suggested.

'Can't go to a pub and not have chips,' said Frankie. 'Yeah. And a sandwich. The ham, I think.'

Sandy got up to order and Frankie offered her money.

'Oh no, we'll pay at the end,' Sandy assured her.

She returned quickly and upon sitting down,

immediately asked, 'So, Frankie, what do you do? Other than renovate properties. Or is that your job?'

Frankie blinked.

'Oh, erm, yeah. I'm sort of in the midst of a career change right now. So I guess I'm trying the property route.'

'What did you do before?'

Frankie swallowed and found her mouth achingly dry. She reached for her lemonade and took two gulps, which swirled around her empty stomach.

'I, erm, did a lot of travelling. Between the UK and the US. I had to quit. Turns out I hate flying.' She gave a small laugh which turned into a little hiccup and Frankie snapped her mouth shut.

Sandy gave her a strange look.

'Sounds fancy. What were you doing in the US?'

Frankie sighed.

'Acting. I was an actor.'

Sandy's eyes widened.

'In LA?'

Frankie nodded and Sandy's eyes widened further.

'And you were successful? I mean, enough to buy and renovate in the London property market, and to buy the local farmhouse. My boss went to view it, you know. I know how much it was up for, and it must be costing a few hundred thousand to renovate.'

'Not quite...'

'Even so, that's probably a million right there.' Sandy leaned forward and lowered her voice. 'So, what have you been in? Anything I'd know?'

Frankie thought quick, searching Sandy's large, pleading eyes. Then she sighed, relenting.

'Maybe,' she murmured. 'How are you with superhero films?'

Sandy squeaked and clapped a hand over her mouth.

'I played a teleporter in eight of The Defender franchise films,' Frankie explained.

'Oh my god.' Sandy pulled out her phone and began tapping away at the screen.

'What are you doing?'

'Googling you.'

Frankie laughed.

'I'm right here. What would you like to know?'

'Oh my god, it is you!' Sandy held up her phone next to Frankie and looked between them, then showed Frankie the screen. There she was, in her silver wig, posing for a promotional photo for the last film. 'I can't believe it. I'm out to lunch with a Hollywood star.'

'Okay, first of all, yes, I was in those big films, and yes, that's how I'm paying for the house and stuff. But I am absolutely not a Hollywood star and don't you ever call me that again,' Frankie said with a smile, so Sandy wouldn't find it too threatening. 'It was ten years of selling my soul and not getting paid as much as anyone else in those posters.

Thankfully I had other long-term acting jobs, so I vowed not to touch the money I made from those films. I invested it instead, and over ten years of adding to it, it grew and grew. It's always been money for my dream house, so here we are.'

Sandy stared at her.

'That's incredible. But you've quit acting now?'

Frankie nodded.

'Oh, but you must have some stories.'

Frankie laughed.

'Of course. And I'll happily share them, but enough about me. Tell me about you. Do you live locally?'

Sandy nodded, sipping her drink. There was a pause as their food arrived.

'I was born in the next town over but moved here when I got the job at the vets. Been there for six years. Michael bought the practice last year and he convinced me to stay on. I was thinking of finding a job in the city, but it's one hell of a commute compared to falling out of bed and wandering up the high street.'

Frankie nodded, popping a chip in her mouth and then exclaiming how delicious they were.

'Oh, yeah. This place does the best chips,' said Sandy, grinning as she smothered her own chips in tomato sauce.

Frankie considered Sandy as she chewed her mouthful.

'What would you have done in the city?'

Sandy shrugged.

'Probably some boring receptionist job in a big office building with no dogs or cats or rats or guinea pigs.' She shuddered. 'Just the idea makes me want to scream.'

'You've always loved animals?'

Sandy nodded.

'Michael keeps suggesting I train as a nurse. Or a vet.' She grinned. 'I can't afford to become a vet, and nursing is a little full on. I just like being organised and giving out cuddles.'

Frankie smiled.

'Sounds like you're in just the right job.'

'Yep. And Michael keeps things interesting. Although he's not always here. He's got the practice he inherited from his father in the city, and the charity work. The man doesn't stop. No wonder he's single.' Sandy took a big bite of her sandwich. 'Are you single?' she asked around the food.

Frankie stared down at her own food and nodded.

'Yeah. Have been for a while. Broke up with my last boyfriend because he didn't want to move to the UK from New York. Which I can't blame him, because I didn't want to move permanently to New York.'

'Why not? I'd love a man to sweep me off my feet and move me to New York.'

Frankie gave a sad smile.

'New York isn't what everyone makes it out to be.

It's like London. It's got lots of nice places and big fancy dreams, but in reality it's dirty, too full of people and there are so many rats.'

She expected Sandy to pull a face, but instead, Sandy grinned.

'I know. I love rats.'

Frankie tilted her head to the side and chuckled.

'Well, maybe being swept out to New York would be right for you, then.'

Sandy nodded.

'Are you with anyone?' Frankie asked.

Again, Sandy nodded.

'School sweetheart. He's a gardener, studying to become a landscape designer at the local college.'

'Ooh, interesting.'

'Yeah, but everything's this plant this and that flower that. Although he does do a lot for the local wildlife, too.'

'Does he know much about trees?'

Sandy nodded and put three chips in her mouth.

'He did an arboriculture course last year. Why?'

'The farmhouse came with the edge of a little woodland and I want to make sure it's healthy, and maybe expand it a little.'

Sandy's eyes widened again.

'Yes! He'd love that. I'll give you his number.'

Frankie beamed and they fell into conversation about the local college and the local wildlife, and Sandy's New York dreams of being whisked away by a landscape designer.

Eight

It was half eight when Michael made it home. Agnes was waiting and immediately turned her back on him.

'I know, I know. I'm sorry I'm so late,' he told her, hanging up his coat and pulling off his woollen hat and scarf. 'It's been a day.' He wandered through his flat and into the kitchen, reaching for the bottle of wine in the fridge, having already ordered food on his way home. He poured himself a glass and then fed Agnes. His usual evening shower to wash the day away would have to wait. 'I was in Bekburn this morning and was meant to be there all day, but an emergency came into the city practice in the early afternoon. Not ideal, I know, but I had to be there. We ended up going into surgery for four hours, then all the paperwork and admin and other consultations on top of that.' Michael collapsed into an armchair, taking care not to spill his wine. 'I know what Dad would say,' he continued, stroking Agnes as she jumped into his lap; forgiveness came quick, as long as there was food. 'I'm spreading myself too thin. I need to start delegating more. I should pick a practice, stick with it, and hire a head vet for the other one.' Michael sighed. 'But how to choose which practice?'

Reow, said Agnes, looking up at him with the type of expression he could imagine his mother giving him.

As if somehow hearing his thoughts, his phone burst into life, flashing Mum on the screen.

'How does she do that?' Michael muttered before answering. 'Hi, Mum.'

'Nine down, a comic book franchise owned by famous ears. I would ask if the king likes comic books, but that seems unlikely and apparently six down contains an "F", third letter, which ruins that idea.'

Michael smiled.

'I don't know, Mum. Maybe Jamie would know.'

He could hear his mother counting on her fingers.

'He'll be asleep still or busy getting the kids up. Are you all right? You sound tired.'

'Yeah, I'm fine. Just a busy day, that's all.' Michael gave Agnes a look that told her not to breathe a word that he'd only just come home from work. 'I've been made aware that I might need to delegate to a head vet at one of the practices.'

Michael cringed as his mother burst into laughter.

'Oh, Michael. Oh, I'm sorry, my love. But, yes! This is only occurring to you now? In fact, didn't I make this exact suggestion when you bought the rural practice?'

Michael sighed gently through his nose.

'Yes. You did.'

'Hmm. I think it's a wonderful idea. You're doing too much. You always have. You should delegate more than the running of one practice, you know. Why not find two head vets, one for each practice? Cut back on your work hours, enjoy some living instead.'

'I guess if I did that, I could do more for the charity. Set up a proper practice for drop-ins and surgery while still going to meet people on the streets.'

'No, Michael, that's a third practice you're talking yourself into. You're not listening. You. Need. To. Slow. Down.'

'Why, Mum?'

'Because... Because you're not... Are you enjoying life?'

Michael gave this some consideration and the pause was enough for his mother.

'Aha! Last time I asked that, you said yes immediately. Were you lying then? Or has something changed?'

'I thought that the reason I didn't make an offer on that farmhouse in Bekburn was because it was too large, but actually now I wonder if it was just because I don't know where I want to be,' he blurted.

'Hmm. Something's pulling you to that farmhouse, even though it wasn't enough to put an offer on it when you had the chance.'

Michael watched Agnes as she leapt up to sit on the top of his piano and clean her paws.

'I don't want to leave the city. I would like to do more for the charity, that's not a lie.'

This time, his mother sighed.

'My darling boy,' she murmured. 'You've always carried such a weight around with you. And you never needed to. Your father didn't need you to take over the practice, he was happy as long as you were happy. You didn't have to follow him.'

Michael frowned.

'But I wanted to. I enjoy it. I enjoy every aspect of it. Except for the paperwork and admin and chemical smell and rude people.'

Esme laughed.

'Well, there's not much that can be done about rude people that you're not already doing. But here's an idea. This month, December, is the last month where you do everything. I want you to stop working over Christmas, take some proper time off and have a really good think about what you want and where you want to be. Then, in January, employ at least two head vets and a personal assistant for yourself. Make sure your practice managers don't need assistants, too. If they do, hire them.'

'And how am I going to pay all of their salaries?' Michael asked, although he couldn't deny that it was a nice idea. Something he wouldn't have considered a year before.

'Oh, don't give me that. I know you. You'll have been saving since your father left us. And he saved before that. I bet there's a good pot of money for this kind of thing. You just have to be willing to put that money to good use.'

'And what if there's an emergency? That's what that money is for. Dad never needed a head vet and even his practice manager was part time.'

'And what exactly do you think I did, Michael?' came Esme's stern response.

Michael opened his mouth and then slowly closed it.

'You did Dad's admin?'

'Yes.'

Michael smiled.

'Is this why you tell me I need to find a wife?'

'Heavens, no! Don't put the woman you love through that. I did it for your father because I offered, and because he refused to hire someone to help. Learn from him. Hire someone. You don't need a wife for that, you need a good administrative professional. If you happen to fall in love with them, then that's fine, but get your priorities straight.'

Michael laughed.

'Have you, erm, met anyone recently?' Esme asked, her voice suddenly quieter.

An image of the dark-haired woman who owned the farmhouse sprang into Michael's mind. He still didn't know her name. He could only guess at her surname, given than her mother had registered their dog at the practice. Still, he'd dreamt about her twice, saw her in the city once, and was acutely aware that Sandy had been having lunch with her across the road from the rural practice when he'd received the call about the city emergency case.

'No,' he said, and heard his mother's expression change to one of suspicion. 'Well...'

'Well?'

'No.'

'Michael.'

He sighed and rubbed at his tired eyes.

'The woman who bought the farmhouse.'

'Yes?'

'She's... I saw her in the city the other day. She walked past me when I was with a client. And I...' Michael snapped his mouth shut. He could hardly tell his mother that he'd been having sordid dreams about this woman before he even met her.

'And you...?'

Michael pursed his lips.

'It doesn't matter. It's probably more regret that I didn't put in an offer for the farmhouse.'

Esme tutted.

'Rubbish. What's she like?'

'Beautiful.' Michael pressed his lips together and then blew out his cheeks thoughtfully. 'She seems very nice.'

'What's her name?'

'I don't know.'

'What do you mean, you don't know? Have you never spoken to her? How do you know if she's nice?'

'I've spoken to her. She brought her parents' dog in to see me, but she didn't register the dog. I know her mother's surname, but that doesn't mean it's her name. And I don't know her first name. Sandy had lunch with her today.'

'So Sandy knows her name?'

'Well, yes.'

'And have you asked Sandy?'

'No...'

'Michael.'

'Mum, I'm not going to stalk the poor woman. You asked if I've met anyone and that's my answer. No. I haven't.'

'But the woman who bought the house you were coveting is beautiful?'

'Well, yes. But don't put it like that.'

'Why not?'

'Because I didn't covet the house.'

'So, it's not about you wanting the woman who bought the house, then, is it? It's just about the woman.'

Michael stopped. Damn her.

'Jamie's already double dared me to ask her out,' he said quietly.

Esme laughed so loud that Michael flinched and had to move the phone away from his ear.

'Of course he has, and for once, I agree with him. No! I triple dare you!' Esme cackled until Michael couldn't help but grin.

'Fine. Thank you for that.'

The doorbell rang, making Agnes look up sharply and then fix her eyes on Michael.

'I have to go, Mum. My food's just arrived.'

'What? What do you mean? It's nearly nine o'clock!'

'Yeah...'

'Oh, Michael. When did you finish work?'

Damn. Michael clenched his eyes shut for a moment and then responded to the video doorbell to let the delivery driver know he'd be right down. Grabbing his keys, he ventured out to the stairs.

'It's not like me getting home at half eight is a regular thing, Mum. We had an emergency surgery case come in. And I've come home and immediately thought about hiring a head vet. Okay?'

'I suppose. Please do hire someone. Get the job adverts written and out now. Maybe hold the interviews before Christmas. Please? Next year has to be different, Michael. Working this hard can't be doing you any good. I don't want you to regret not having lived your life. Look at your brother!'

Michael had been waiting for that. She always

managed to bring up Jamie when she was admonishing Michael's life choices, even when he knew she was trying really hard not to.

'I know, Mum.'

'I mean, please don't move to Australia. I'm so very glad you're still in Scotland, but, sweetheart… Buy a place in Bekburn, move out of the city, meet new people, try new things. And then we'll go for coffee and cake and you can tell me all about it.'

Michael smiled.

'Of course,' he said. 'I will. I'll sort it out. Next year will be different.'

'Promise?'

'I have to go, Mum. Have a good night. Speak to you later?'

'Fine. Love you.'

'Love you, Mum,' said Michael, standing next to the door. He hung up, opened the door and retrieved his food. By the time he'd made it back upstairs to his flat, a message had pinged up on his phone. He sighed, expecting it to be his mother, and was relieved to find it was his best friend from university, Dane.

Hey! Haven't heard from you in ages. Everything okay? Milly wants to know if you're seeing anyone? I'll give you one guess why.

Michael laughed to himself and put the phone down in order to dish up his food. He made himself comfortable in his armchair, plate heaped high on his lap and a glass of red wine on the side table. Agnes came over to investigate but Michael pushed her away.

'You've had yours, this is mine. Go away.'

Agnes gave him a glare and moved back to watch him eat. Picking up his phone, he replied to his old friend.

Hey. Sorry about that. Been busy. Hopefully next year will be different – going to be hiring some more staff over the next few months. And tell Milly thank you but no thank you, I don't want to be set up on another blind date.

Michael found the TV remote on the table. He flicked through the channels, chewing slowly.

She says you'll change your mind when you meet this woman she's found. Great stuff about hiring more staff. Maybe we can play more golf next year?

Having left the TV on some dark crime drama, Michael turned his attention back to his phone to reply, his heart pounding at the idea of expanding the practices further. Before, the idea had made him queasy, but now there was a hint of excitement. It hadn't occurred to him that it would also free him up to see more of Dane out on the golf course.

Can't remember the last time we played golf! That would be great. Let's book it in. And tell Milly that I won't, but thanks all the same. How are you doing?

Pulling a face, Michael flicked across some more channels. He passed on a reality show, a comedy show and a programme about two celebrities walking on a beach and explaining how wonderful it was.

We're all good, mate. No news here. Other than Milly's sure she's met the woman of your dreams. How about we go to the driving range. Are you around before Christmas?

An image of the woman who owned the farmhouse sprang back into Michael's mind. The literal woman of his dreams. He smiled.

I doubt she has. I can make myself available before Christmas. When were you thinking?

Michael turned off the TV and shovelled another forkful of food into his mouth, his eyelids already heavy.

Why so much doubt? You never know. We should all get together before Christmas anyway.

Drinks? The Friday before?

Michael narrowed his eyes.

Just you, me and Milly. Right?

He watched his phone's screen as the three dots came up.

Sure. But next week if you're up for proving Milly wrong?

Michael grinned and stopped the laugh bubbling up that would have sprayed food over his plate.

I can prove her wrong in other ways. Yes to the Friday before. No to the date. Yes to the driving range but maybe not until January?

Michael took another two mouthfuls before he stared down at his food, considering if he could save the rest for tomorrow night.

Perfect. Will have a go at calming Milly down. And will get some January dates for golf. Night!

Michael sent a message saying good night, and then ventured back to the kitchen to save half of his meal. It wasn't that he wasn't hungry or that the food wasn't good, but exhaustion had hit him like a brick wall. He tidied up, put everything away, made sure Agnes had fresh water, and then turned off the lights. He made sure his shower was hot and stood underneath it, feeling the knots in his back loosen, before he dried himself off and slipped into bed, falling immediately into a deep sleep and wondering as he went if the dark-haired woman would visit him again that night.

Nine

'Do you know, I've not had a mince pie yet,' said Irene as Frankie stepped off the tram with her. They were at St Andrews Square and Frankie stopped to look around.

'I can buy some from M&S if you like?' she offered as her mother pulled out her phone to look at the directions. In front of them was the square, with the impossibly tall, grey statue on a column in the centre. Frankie had always assumed the statue to be of St Andrew, given the name of the square, but had recently discovered that it was actually the statue of an eighteenth-century politician with dubious beliefs, so she was glad of the seagull excrement covering his head and the fact that the column was so tall she couldn't make out his features. The square's garden had been put to sleep for the winter and a couple of shacks where children could write their letter to Santa and actually meet Santa had been put up. Staff milled around, waiting for families, and inside the letter writing shack, a small child was busy staring thoughtfully at a piece of paper. Around the square, a blue double decker bus giving tours of the city followed the road until it reached the top of the square and stopped, dropping people off and picking others up.

'That might be nice,' said Irene, distracted.

'Which way are you heading?' Frankie asked, trying to look over her mother's shoulder to the information on her phone.

'This way.' Irene pointed through the square, to the street and buildings opposite.

'Okay. I'll walk with you.'

They walked side by side through the square, following the path around the lawn and monument, where they crossed the road and walked past another statue that also wasn't of St Andrew. Either side, beautiful old buildings loomed over them, although the road was wide enough that there was parking in the centre. They wandered past a church and banks and cafés and imposing buildings with columns at their entrances, and Frankie and Irene marvelled at it all.

'I can't believe we live so close to all this,' Irene murmured. She gave her daughter a sideways look. 'Do you regret not buying somewhere central?'

'No,' said Frankie, surprising herself by meaning it. 'I don't think Lily is a city dog, is she? And Dad isn't a city man. They both need the gardens and trees. Plus, have you seen our driveway? It's ridiculous. Pretty much a sweeping driveway. I was thinking last night, I could put a giant Christmas tree in the middle of it. That would make it sweeping, wouldn't it? I could plant a small tree and we can watch it grow or I could pay to have a giant one installed every year.'

Irene laughed.

'Well, we both know what you're going to do. And I'm sure your dad will love helping you to plant it.'

Frankie grinned, straining her neck back to look up at the buildings. They reached another cross-roads with yet another statue and Frankie guessed it likely that he wasn't St Andrew either.

'I go right here and then wander along a little further. The workshop is at a gallery down there somewhere. I should be done in a few hours. Where shall I meet you?'

'I'll probably head up to Princes Street Gardens,' mused Frankie. 'We could meet back here? Or give me the address and I'll come find you? Or meet back at the tram stop?'

'Let's meet back at the square. In about three and a half hours.'

Irene checked her watch and Frankie looked at the time on her phone. They gave one another a quick hug and parted ways. Hands deep in her pockets, Frankie turned her back on the way her mother was walking and headed for Princes Street, where she crossed the road and wandered past the national galleries and up the Mound. At the top, she paused, partly to catch her breath and partly to decide which way she should go up to the Royal Mile.

'Screw it,' she murmured, turning right and starting the steep ascent up towards the castle. She regretted her decision after less than a minute, but continued nonetheless. A part of her – the part that wasn't fighting for air or cursing all the time she'd wasted not working out – wondered if she should have asked to join her mother at the painting workshop. It was an introductory session to painting with oils, something her mother had never done and Frankie hadn't done since a failed attempt at a hobby during her university years. It would do her good to try new things, but her mother would never have agreed. How were they going to meet new people and make friends if they just did things together?

Frankie made it to the top of the Royal Mile and swallowed hard, trying to appear fit and healthy as she joined the throng of tourists. She glanced up towards the castle esplanade, but turned away from it and headed down the famous high street. There were no Christmas lights on the Royal Mile, but the whisky experience had their tree up and decorated outside, and the shop windows were festooned with lights and fake snow. The roads coming off the high street had Christmas lights sweeping from buildings on one side of the road to the other and back again, lighting up the gloom that was a drizzly

Edinburgh early afternoon.

Pulling her hat lower over her ears, Frankie considered where to go next. Three hours was a long time, so she should stop at a coffee shop somewhere. Or perhaps do a little sightseeing.

The drizzle turned to rain and Frankie shivered.

She knew the sights. She'd been a tourist often enough, it was time to act like a resident. Striding down the Royal Mile, she dodged the clumps of tourists and their umbrellas, before diving into a Starbucks and standing a moment to appreciate the warmth that hit her.

She ordered a hot chocolate and slice of cake and took her prizes to a table recently vacated near the back, looking out through a large window to the Royal Mile and the rain that was steadily falling harder. The glass was steaming up, but Frankie could still see enough to people watch. She peeled off her thick coat, aware that it was dripping, yanked off her hat and smoothed down her hair. Then she huddled over the hot drink and ate her cake, watching people hurry past, guessing easily who was finishing off their lunch break and who was on holiday. By the time her plate was empty except for a few crumbs, Frankie caught herself staring down at it, absent-mindedly sipping the last of the hot chocolate.

She felt sick.

Her mind, however, was not on her stomach but on her bank account. The move to London, three years previous, had been about starting a new life and maybe a new career. She'd bought a Victorian terrace in dire need of love and set about breathing new life into it with a complete restoration and renovation. It had been fun. She'd ended up retiling the kitchen, bathroom and downstairs toilet, using videos from YouTube to teach herself. Her parents had pointed out that she'd always been interested in property, even buying herself a small apartment in LA when her acting career started to take off. She argued that she only bought that apartment so she didn't have to waste money on hotels all the time, but eventually she had to agree with her parents; she had enjoyed turning that all white apartment into a blast of colour and personality. The real estate agent had been less thrilled, but Frankie hadn't wanted to make money on it. That apartment had been a means to an end, and when it ended, she was happy to break even. The Victorian terrace, on the other hand, had made her a tidy sum, thanks to the extension, loft conversion and London property market. She had no plans to sell the Scottish farmhouse and its little cottage. As far as Frankie was concerned, this was the forever dream home.

That didn't mean she couldn't invest in other property, though. Frankie sighed gently through her nose. The property market was in crisis. The last thing Frankie wanted was to become a landlord, squeezing pennies out of her tenants and giving them a property that made them ill. No, if she was to become a landlord, her properties would be modern, fresh, beautiful and eco-friendly. That would cost, but what else was she going to spend those zeroes on?

After her first major feature film, Frankie had put the money aside and invested it for the sole purpose of retirement one day. The second film's salary was also stashed away ready to buy her a modest dream house. That was all she needed. She had enough to keep her alive and happy for the extent of a long, full life. Unable to turn down the rest of the films due to the contract she'd signed, the money that had followed had seemed like a blessing.

Frankie had to be the only person to become a multi-millionaire and feel so guilty and down about it. She shook her head. Of course she wasn't the only person, but she had to change how she felt. She needed to rid herself of the guilt. And the only way to do that was to help people.

Lifting her eyes to the damp Royal Mile, Frankie considered the possibility of creating a property portfolio of affordable rental homes across the UK A smile touching her lips, Frankie pulled on her still dripping coat, dragged her hat over her head and ears, and strode out of the warmth of the coffee shop. The chill of outside hit her, sending shivers through her wet hat and down into her body. Pulling off the hat, she stuffed it into her coat pocket and pulled up her hood instead. It wasn't raining anymore, at least, and the hood did something to keep the warmth in. Frankie headed back up the high street to gaze in shop windows and venture inside one or two, checking the time as she went. As she slid her phone back into her pocket, she glanced up and her heart jolted.

The vet – Michael – met her eyes, seemingly froze and then turned sharply, becoming overly interested in the nearest shop window. After a moment, he dug his hands into his coat pockets and strode down the road, past her on the other side, not so much as glancing at her. Frankie watched him, waiting to catch his eye again, to maybe wave. Would he recognise her? Would he remember her? Apparently not. She was sure that he had seen her, but he ignored her.

Her heart still pounding, her mouth dry, Frankie gave a little growl at herself. Why did she do this? One attractive man and she started dithering. Given the time she'd spent with so many men that other women drooled over, she'd thought she'd be used to it. The only times she'd acted like this was when she'd met someone she was undeniably attracted to, and none of those men had been famous actors, or even directors, producers or writers. They'd been camera operators, sound engineers, the chef of a catering company. And now, apparently, a veterinarian.

Frankie tutted to herself. She had everything she

wanted: the dream house, enough money to live a luxurious life, the love of her parents and Lily, and the beginnings of a new dream. She didn't need a man. Especially one who ignored her, and who she'd probably have to see again next time Lily needed medical care or her annual check-up. All being well, she might only see Michael once a year, and that's only if her parents didn't want to take Lily to the vets.

Frankie frowned and went to find another café to solve her dry mouth and throat. Preferably one that sold mince pies. She'd look up properties for sale in the city centre, just out of interest, a spot of light research, and then she'd go meet her mother. There would be no more thinking about men.

Ten

Furious with himself, Michael marched all the way down to Holyrood and stood outside the Parliament building. Apart from anything else, he'd come the wrong way. He'd meant to walk back up the Royal Mile to look in a couple of shops for ideas of what to buy his mother for Christmas. Instead, he'd somehow looked up at the exact moment the dark-haired woman had met his eyes, walking towards him. Panic had filled every part of his body – well, not every part – and his legs had gone into flight mode, dragging him all the way down to the end of the road in the wrong direction.

He glanced at the uniformed police officer standing close to the Parliament entrance, then turned his attention to Arthur's Seat. Taking in a deep breath, Holyrood Park in front of him and the city at his back, Michael's heart began to calm.

Was this ever going to go away? He'd dreamt about this woman twice, and now he'd seen her in the city twice. He didn't even know her name.

Maybe if he found out her name, this would stop. Maybe if he met someone else, this would stop.

Michael fretted for a moment and then pulled out his phone, ambling back up the Royal Mile as he messaged Dane.

Hey. Tell Milly I've changed my mind. Let's do that date.

He'd come to regret it. He already regretted it, the moment he hit send. But there was always the chance that his friends would come through, that they'd introduce him to the woman of his dreams and he would finally be able to leave the literal woman from his dreams behind. Michael ignored the ache in his gut that went against everything he was thinking, and stopped at a Starbucks to grab a takeaway coffee.

In his pocket, his phone vibrated.

You sure, mate? What changed your mind?

Michael replied as he waited for his drink to be made.

Just the idea of what if.

He stared at the message before he hit send, his mind flitting back to the dark-haired woman. What if.

Michael shook his head and thanked the barista for his coffee, pushing open the door back into the cold, damp December day. He had just enough time to check out a couple of shops on his way back to his practice, if he was quick.

The next morning, Michael was running late. He'd been up late the night before writing out the job description for the head vet vacancy and making lists of everything he'd need to delegate. It had been exhausting. He'd sent the email to his HR manager with everything attached at quarter to midnight and promptly fallen into bed. Having woken with a start at six, Michael had sleepily checked his calendar for that day, his phone screen lighting up his bedroom. It was so dark that if he hadn't seen the time, he wouldn't have believed it was morning. The cloud had to be thick in the sky, blocking out whatever little light there would usually be.

His first appointment in his rural practice wasn't until ten o'clock. Bless Sandy and her knowing ways, she was worth every penny of the pay rise he'd given her upon buying the practice, and more. He'd wondered for a moment if she'd be interested in a promotion but had fallen back to sleep before the thought could grow, and of course he'd fallen back to sleep not having reset his alarm.

Still, the sleep had done him good. He woke

naturally to daylight, fed a purring Agnes, played O Come, All Ye Faithful on the piano, said goodbye to the cat and drove contentedly out of the city and into Bekburn at nine o'clock with something resembling a smile on his face. When he parked the car, he glanced at his phone and found a message waiting for him from his mother.

Can you pop round this evening with a few bottles of wine? It's book club tonight and it's so cold.

Michael almost laughed. Staying in the warmth of his car, he called his mother.

'You didn't have to call. A simple yes would have sufficed,' said Esme.

'Good morning, Mum. Hello to you, too. Are you possibly playing the old lady card?'

Esme laughed.

'Good morning, Michael. Hello. Bonjour. I might be. It's also a sneaky mother tactic to make her son leave work at a reasonable time. Book club is at eight, don't be late.'

'You're not expecting me to stay at book club, are you?'

'Only if you want to. You don't have to. We have a new trial member coming, so I need to make sure we have plenty of wine.'

'Oh. I didn't know you took on new members.'

'Why wouldn't we?'

Michael stopped and gave this some thought,

imagining his mother and all her friends gathered in a room, lounging on sofas, drinking wine.

'I guess because I didn't think you actually discussed books.'

'Whether we discuss books or not at book club is not the point, Michael. The point is that we're always open to meeting new friends and she's been made well aware that there will be wine and that it doesn't matter if she hasn't actually read the actual book.' Esme cleared her throat. 'I don't know how much more obvious about it all I can be.'

Michael caught himself grinning.

'What sort of things do you talk about? Or do I not want to know?'

'Oh, nothing much. The usual. Why, are you tempted to come and stay?'

'Oh no, but I will drop off some wine. How is that?'

'Thank you. You're so very good at looking after your poor, ageing mother.'

'Hmm.' Michael shook his head.

'Are you all right?'

'Of course. Why?'

'You're smiling. I can hear it.'

'And... That means something is wrong?' Michael asked, checking out his own smile in the rear view mirror.

'Well, no. But something is different. Have you asked out that woman yet?'

Michael's reflected smile turned into an awkward frown and he turned away from the mirror.

'No.'

He could feel his mother's expression: her eyes narrowing, a smile touching the corners of her lips.

'You hesitated, Michael. And that was a rather strangled "no".'

'Was it? Did I?'

'Hmm. Why haven't you asked her?'

Michael's stomach flipped and he put a hand over it questioningly.

'I haven't, erm, had the chance.'

He could practically hear his mother raising her eyebrows.

'Anyway, I have a date with someone else.' His stomach turned as he said the words.

'Oh? Who is she?'

'A friend of Dane and Milly's.'

'You sound thrilled about it.'

Michael sighed.

'I'm sure it'll be great,' he said, not believing a word of it. 'I've got to go, Mum. I'm seeing a client soon.'

'Okay, well, take care and remember, wine at eight, don't—'

'—Be late,' Michael joined in. 'I got it. I'll see you before eight, how's that?'

'Perfect.'

They said their goodbyes and hung up. Michael left his car and entered the practice, his gaze immediately finding Sandy at the reception desk.

She was on the phone but just finishing up and gave Michael a warm grin as he approached. The waiting room was practically empty, with just one woman and a cat carrier waiting.

'Is that my ten o'clock?' Michael whispered.

'No. She's got a nurse appointment.'

Michael nodded, relieved that he still had time to settle and have a quick coffee.

'Thank you, Sandy,' he started, giving the receptionist a stray look as he tried to get the words out with just the right tone. 'Oh! Erm, that cocker spaniel's owner. Lily, wasn't it? What was the name of the woman who brought her in?'

'Lily Taylor? I'm not sure of her owners' names.' Sandy gave Michael a sideways look and he pretended to check through a file on Sandy's desk.

'Their daughter brought her in. For a check-up and her boosters. What was her name again?'

Sandy nodded.

'Francesca Taylor. But it's Frankie. I had lunch with her.'

'Frankie,' Michael whispered accidentally out loud. He snapped his mouth shut, heart pounding, half wondering if now his brain would forget about Frankie Taylor and knowing, deep down in his gut, that if anything, he'd just made the whole thing worse.

He stopped when he realised Sandy was looking up at him with a silly grin.

'What?' he asked, his legs already turning him

around so he could run to his office and escape.

'Do you know who she is?'

Michael's legs hesitated.

'What? She's the woman who bought the farmhouse. Isn't she?'

'Oh, yeah, but do you know who she is?'

Sandy gave something of a gleeful cackle at Michael's confused expression.

'Look!' She opened a new window on her computer and pulled up YouTube, quickly typing in Frankie's full name. A number of videos came up and Michael edged closer, peering at each in turn.

'I don't understand,' he murmured.

'Just wait for it.' Sandy opened one of the videos and pressed play. 'C'mon, c'mon,' she muttered as an advert played. She hit the skip button as soon as it appeared and then sat back as they watched what appeared to be a scene from a superhero film.

'I still don't understand,' said Michael, his back beginning to ache from bending over to see the screen properly.

Sandy paused the video and pointed at one of the actors, a woman with long silver hair, wearing jeans and a hoody, her hands in her pockets.

'That is Frankie Taylor.'

The floor fell away from Michael. He saw it now. Replace the silver with dark hair and suddenly it was hard to miss her eyes, those lips, the way she held herself. That smile.

Michael caught himself smiling.

'She's a Hollywood actor,' said Sandy, grinning up at him. 'Can you believe it? She explained everything over lunch. She quit acting a few years ago and moved to London, then decided to follow her dream of living in Scotland, so here she is. She was waiting to find a man to share her life with, but gave up and dragged her parents up here instead. They're living in the cottage that came with the farmhouse. She's really lovely. So friendly. Not at all what I expected from a Hollywood actor. And you see him?' – Sandy pointed to a dark-haired, chiselled man standing beside Frankie on the screen – 'I've had a crush on him for about six years, and she knows him! Scared my boyfriend when I told him that. Can you imagine? A Hollywood star in our little town, and she's so nice. And she went to lunch with me!' Sandy gave a little squeal and then made a show of calming herself. 'Of course, we must not act like this in front of her. I need to get all of my fangirl screams out when she's not here.'

When Michael didn't respond, Sandy looked back up to him. 'Are you all right, boss?'

'Hmm? Oh, yes. Very...interesting.' Michael swallowed hard, now in desperate need of that coffee.

Sandy pressed play on the video and they watched the rest of the scene in silence. Michael flinched.

'What happened then?' he asked, his voice

cracking.

'She plays a teleporter. So her character just teleported. Disappeared in a cloud of smoke. Cool, huh?'

'Oh, yeah. Cool,' said Michael. 'Very interesting. Very. Thank you, erm, Sandy. I'd best go and...get ready for my first client.'

'Yes, ten o'clock. I'll let you know when they're here.'

'Thanks.' Blankly, Michael turned from the reception desk and found his way to the kitchen, made a coffee, and then closed the door on his office and slumped into his chair.

Frankie.

It was a beautiful name, he decided, and suited her well.

Michael and Frankie had a nice ring to it, or so the little voice in the back of his head pointed out. He sipped his coffee with trembling fingers.

She was a Hollywood actor, working alongside big names. He knew of the man Sandy had pointed out, knew how famous he was, although Michael couldn't for the life of him remember the man's name.

A Hollywood actor with a Hollywood salary. What on earth would she want with a dowdy, lanky vet in Scotland?

An ache grew in Michael's chest at the thought. He shook his head and took a gulp of hot coffee, grimacing at the burning in his throat as the pain from the coffee overtook the ache that Frankie would never be attracted to someone like him.

Not that it mattered.

He'd wanted to forget about her, to stop these strange feelings, and this was the answer. He had a date with another woman to focus on. Not to mention his work.

Michael ran a hand down his face. Focus on the work, he told himself. Focus on the work, and on this date, and nothing else.

Ten minutes later, he realised he hadn't moved, his coffee was cold, and the image of Frankie meeting his eyes wouldn't budge from his mind.

Eleven

'I'm not sure about this.'

'What are you talking about, Mum? This'll be great!' Frankie looked up at the beautiful, large Victorian semi-detached house she'd managed to park near. 'You're sure it's that one?'

Irene checked the address again and nodded.

'Yes, that's the one. Number forty-two.'

Frankie watched her mother struggle.

'What's wrong?' she asked gently. 'You've been to all these new things since we moved up here and I haven't seen you like this once.'

Irene shuffled in her seat, staring up at the houses they were parked beside.

'Those were workshops. You know, go into the back room of a gallery or somewhere, sit down, make small talk until the teacher comes in. This is...different.'

'Because it's someone's house?' Frankie looked back up at the semi-detached. There was a small Christmas tree in the front window, the glowing lights adding a welcoming warmth to the building. 'It looks like a lovely house.'

Irene began wringing her hands, leaving the book she'd brought in her lap.

'What if a murderer lives there?' she whispered, barely audible.

Frankie studied her mother.

'What if I come in with you?' she offered. 'Safety in numbers, right?'

Irene glanced at her and then shook her head.

'If there's a murderer in there, I don't want to put you in danger.'

Frankie smiled.

'Is that a murder mystery you read for this?' She gestured to the book in her mother's lap.

'Yes. What's your point?'

Frankie laughed.

'Come on, or you'll be late. I'll walk with you to the door, at least.' Frankie opened the car door and stepped out. There came the quiet slam of her mother climbing out the passenger side and closing the door, then Irene scurried around the car to join Frankie on the pavement.

'Deep breath,' she whispered, and Frankie reached out and took her hand. As they started approaching the house, a figure strode down the path from the front door and turned right, walking ahead of them. Their head was down, hands in their pockets, but their height and general outline made Frankie's heart jolt. She admonished herself silently. Not everyone of that height and shape would be Michael the vet. Chewing on her lower lip, she checked the house number for the umpteenth time before leading her mother up the path and steps to the front door.

'Ready?'

Irene nodded.

Frankie knocked on the same door that the figure had just walked out of, so wasn't too surprised when it was opened almost immediately.

An older woman, perhaps ten or so years older than Irene, stood before them. Her silver-grey hair was tied up in a messy bun and she was wearing a stunning blue velvet dress. There were thick Christmas-themed bed socks on her feet and a glass of red wine in her hand. Her light blue eyes, behind thick glasses, moved from Frankie to Irene, and she beamed a smile, those eyes lighting up.

'Irene?'

'Yes, hello. I'm Irene.' Frankie's mother stepped forward and cleared her throat. 'This is my daughter, Frankie. I know she's not invited, but she said she'd bring me to the door, just in case—' Irene quickly shut her mouth.

The woman laughed enough that Frankie started smiling.

'Just in case I was a murderer?' she asked in a soft Edinburgh accent. 'Of course! One can never be too careful. I'm Esme and you're both very welcome. Did you drive?' Esme looked over Frankie's shoulder to the road.

'Yes, I'm parked just there.' Frankie pointed. 'I'm probably in someone's way, so...'

'Nonsense! If you leave, you won't get that space back again. Best you come in. We drink wine at these things, but I'm sure I can find something else for a driver. Come on in.' Esme stepped aside.

Irene and Frankie exchanged a look and had what Frankie considered to be a silent conversation and agreement, but then Irene grinned and stepped inside, leaving Frankie behind, which wasn't what she thought they'd agreed. Irene wandered into the house and Esme turned back to Frankie.

'Would you like to join us? You don't have to have read the book. And there's cake.'

Frankie looked to her mother and Irene gave a subtle widening of her eyes. Frankie didn't move, unsure of what that meant.

'Oh, for crying out loud, Frankie, come on in,' Irene laughed, beckoning her daughter inside.

The house was warm with the smell of freshly cooked food, wine and something resembling cinnamon. Frankie and Irene removed their coats and placed them on the hooks Esme pointed out, then Esme gave a quick tour from the hallway.

'Up the stairs, straight ahead, is the toilet, should you need it. The kitchen is through there, should you need it. And we are through here, in the front room. Don't worry about your shoes, but feel free to take them off if you want to. Wine, Irene?'

Esme led the way into the front room where Irene was immediately greeted by the sound of a chorus of women. Smiling to herself, Frankie leaned her head back and studied the period features of the hallway. The curves of the sconces, the ceiling rose around the pendant light, the gleaming wood of the banister, the tiles beneath her feet. Then she remembered herself and rushed after her mother.

'—And this is Frankie, Irene's daughter. It was Frankie, wasn't it?'

Frankie nodded and looked at each of the women in turn, smiling as politely as she could.

'This is Doreen, Faye and Molly.'

They each said hello and Esme gestured to an armchair for Irene and brought a spare dining chair for Frankie.

'Sorry about this. Five is probably our maximum where comfortable chairs are concerned,' Esme murmured.

'Oh, it's no problem,' said Frankie, worried that she should have offered to carry the chair. 'Thank you for including me.'

'Are you both new to Edinburgh?' Doreen asked. She was sitting back on the main sofa of the plush, busy living room. Between the sofa and Esme's armchair was a Victorian fireplace, complete with a real roaring fire, keeping the room perhaps a little too warm. Frankie rolled up the sleeves of her jumper. The walls were painted a deep blue, except for the wall of the chimney breast which featured a wallpaper of deep blues, greens and purples with swirling leaves and exotic birds. Behind Esme's armchair was a bookcase so filled with books that piles were emerging and presumably growing around it. To the other side of the armchair was the small Christmas tree, blinking out of the window and into the Edinburgh evening, framed either side by long, thick purple velvet curtains. The other two women, Molly and Faye, filled the rest of the sofa beside Doreen, who was watching Irene and Frankie with interest.

'Yes. I'm afraid our accents do give us away,' said Irene with a nervous chuckle. 'We're from the South East of England. Near London. Frankie has wanted to live in Scotland for, oh, how long?'

'Over ten years,' Frankie told them. 'Or longer, maybe. I'm not sure. But it's definitely been ten years since I decided I would move up towards Edinburgh one day.'

'It's a beautiful part of the world,' claimed Molly. 'Esme, they don't have drinks.'

'Oh! I'm so sorry. I was just thinking how that dining chair can't be comfortable, but I really don't have another option,' Esme mused, standing and giving Frankie's chair an appraising look. 'There's another armchair upstairs but I can't bring it down. If only my son had stayed a little longer, he could have brought it down. But even then, I think it would take two people.' She met Frankie's eyes. 'You could have brought it down together. Never mind. If you decide to join us more permanently, I'll get him to bring it down next time.'

'I really am fine, thank you,' said Frankie, heat rushing up her neck to her cheeks.

'I'll go fetch another glass. Fill that one, Molly.' Esme pointed to the empty wine glass on the coffee table in the middle of the room and then vanished before Frankie could offer to help.

Molly, a petite woman with blonde hair tied back into a short ponytail, leaned forward to fill Irene's glass with red wine before handing it to her.

'Are you living in Edinburgh?' she asked.

'No, in Bekburn,' said Irene. 'Thank you.' She sipped the wine and then gave it a pleasantly surprised look.

'Oh, yes. Only the best for Esme. It's the next bottle you have to worry about,' Doreen told her. 'Esme ran out so her son just brought over some bottles, and who knows which ones he decided on.'

'Is he good with wine?' Irene asked, and Frankie smiled to herself at the hint of confusion in her mother's voice.

'Definitely not,' said Doreen.

Molly and Faye giggled to themselves and Irene joined in, just as Esme returned.

'Would you like wine, Frankie? Or I have some lemonade in the fridge.'

'One glass won't hurt. I'll sip it slowly. Thank you,' said Frankie.

Irene filled the glass with wine and handed it to

Frankie.

'What have I missed?'

'I was just saying that they have to enjoy this wine, because when this is gone, we're left with what your son brought. Irene asked if he's good with wine.'

Esme smiled.

'It's not one of his talents, no.'

'Bekburn is a bit far, isn't it,' said Molly, settling back. 'Have you been coming into the city often?'

'Bekburn?' asked Esme, taking her seat.

'Yes, that's where they live. Both of you?' Molly checked.

Frankie nodded, but her mother managed to speak first.

'Yes, Frankie bought an old farmhouse on the edge of the town and it came with a cottage. So me and my husband are in the cottage and Frankie has the job of renovating the farmhouse.' Irene sipped more of her wine. 'I did suggest we have the farmhouse, given that there's two of us and one of her, but then I saw the amount of work that needed doing. It's a big job.'

Frankie nodded to herself, her cheeks still burning. She glanced up at the fire, wondering if it was time to remove her jumper, when she realised Esme was staring at her.

'You're the woman who bought the farmhouse in Bekburn,' she murmured.

The heat was no longer because of the fire. All

eyes turned to Frankie and she sank into the dining chair as best she could, her back screaming.

'My son had his eye on that farmhouse. But you're right, Irene. It was far too much work. It put him off. What a shame you just missed him by seconds, I'm sure he would have loved to chat with you. How are you getting on with the renovations?'

The heat lessened as the women returned to their wine and Frankie breathed a little easier.

'Good,' she croaked before clearing her throat. 'Good.'

'She's already getting the tradesmen in. Trying to keep with local tradesmen. If you have any recommendations, I'm sure they wouldn't go amiss,' said Irene.

The heat lessened further as the women murmured amongst themselves, sipping their wine. Frankie glanced at Esme, but the woman had turned her attention to the others.

'Well, Faye's son-in-law has a plumbing business, but otherwise I think we'll be asking you for recommendations,' she said. 'If you can find a tradesman to turn up on time, we'll all want his number.'

The women laughed, and to Frankie it sounded almost like a cackle.

'Well, let's get started, shall we?' Esme leaned forward and picked up her copy of the book from the coffee table. 'First things first, who actually read this?'

'It was very convoluted,' said Doreen. 'I didn't make it past the third chapter.'

'Oh, I read all of it,' said Molly. 'I thought it was brilliant. Lots of violence and murder.'

'Hmm. I remember us agreeing we'd read something gentler. Remember that? I'm sure we talked about it. Maybe the next book can be a romance or drama or anything but crime?' Faye suggested.

'Irene? Did you manage to look at it?' Esme asked.

'I did.' Irene glanced from Doreen to Molly to Faye. 'I quite enjoyed it,' she admitted, and Molly gave a squeal and raised her glass in a toast to Irene.

'I like her. She can stay,' she announced.

Twelve

Michael woke before his alarm went off, reluctantly opening his eyes to the dark. Even Agnes wasn't up on his bed yet. Sleep stayed with him a little longer as he blinked. It was almost as if Frankie was still in the bed with him, her warm skin pressed up against his, her lips on his chest, her thighs straddling him. Michael exhaled a shaky breath as his body continued to respond to the dream that just wouldn't let go of him. He closed his eyes and went back to her long dark hair falling over her pale shoulders, her eyes watching him in the December morning, her pretty smile lowering to kiss his lips.

Agnes leapt onto the bed and swiped at him, and just like that, Frankie Taylor was gone.

Michael ran a hand over his face and groaned. This had to stop. How could he make this stop?

He'd never had dreams like this before. Any dream he'd ever had about a woman, particularly a naked woman, had mostly occurred in his teenage years and early twenties, and not one of them had been as clear and lucid as these dreams. Not one of them had been about a specific woman he knew of, not one had been in such detail.

He hesitated while getting out of bed, wondering for a terrifying and delightful moment if he would discover those details to be true on the chance Frankie ever did go to bed with him.

Shaking his head, Michael scoffed to himself.

Why would Frankie ever agree to go to bed with him? He had no idea how they would get to such a point, never mind why a Hollywood actress would climb the stairs to his Edinburgh flat and fall into his bed.

Michael gave Agnes a sideways look. He'd have to shut the cat out. Michael frowned, trying to remember why he'd never had that thought. Had he not had a relationship since he'd brought Agnes home as a scared and hungry stray? That couldn't be right.

He got up, dressed and fed Agnes her breakfast before feeding himself. Then, with a fresh cup of coffee, he sat at his piano and tinkered with the keys. Agnes jumped onto the top of the piano and sat looking out the window, cleaning her paws as Michael began to play. It was half past seven and still dark, so he played a gentle Christmas hymn as quietly as possible.

At quarter to eight, he finished his coffee, stroked Agnes's ears and left his flat, locking the door behind him and striding down the stairs and out onto the street. By the end of the road, he realised he was smiling and humming Christmas songs, and immediately straightened his lips.

As if in retaliation, his mind conjured the image of Frankie from a selection of the dreams he'd had over the last couple of weeks. All but one had been sex dreams, and even that one had involved a kiss. He could still feel the warmth of it, and once again his body began to respond. Wrapping his coat tighter about him, Michael thought hard of the day ahead until his body seemed to forget Frankie and her soft lips, warm skin and beautiful long hair.

By the time he met Lucia on Princes Street, he was more aware of how cold the day was, despite the rising sun, and the image and feeling of Frankie was gone, hopefully for good.

By midday, Michael had completed his charity work with Lucia, having seen and spoken to eleven people and their pets living rough, including a puppy and a thirteen-year-old Staffordshire bull terrier. Michael's heart went out to both of them and he made a note to spend that evening going over ways he could help those people and their animals further. There had to be a way of getting a roof over their heads, getting them somewhere warm, where the puppy could be a playful baby and the elderly Staffie could relax and dream in peace, safe in the knowledge that their humans were near-by and well.

Shutting the door on his small office in his father's city practice – his city practice – Michael took a moment to scribble down some ideas before he caught himself staring blankly at the wall opposite. With a sigh, he picked up his phone and put it to his ear.

'What time is it there?' Michael laughed as he asked the question, fully aware of the time in Australia and why his brother sounded ruffled.

'You know damn well what time it is.'

'It's hardly the middle of the night,' said Michael. 'It's ten o'clock, isn't it?'

'Half ten. I'm literally sitting on the edge of my bed about to get in. What's up? Is Mum okay?'

'Mum's fine.' Michael leaned back in his chair. 'What are you buying her for Christmas?'

'I don't know. How about we club together and get her plane tickets for you and her to come out here for a visit?'

Michael stopped breathing for a moment, his chest tightening.

'I have to buy my own ticket for Christmas?' His attempt to keep his voice normal failed.

'I was just inviting you,' came Jamie's weary voice. 'You don't have to come. But it's an idea for Mum, right?'

'Right. She'd love that. I think. Not sure about the flying. And the stopover.' Michael chewed his lip. 'Would she be okay with the stopover?'

Jamie sighed down the phone and Michael mentally shook himself. 'No, I know. That's why I was invited.'

'Not the only reason you were invited,' Jamie mumbled. 'You have a niece and nephew who'd like to see you.'

'I know.'

'And it's cheaper to fly you and Mum out here than fly four of us there.'

'Yes.'

'Unless you've met someone you'd like to bring?'

Michael's chest tightened further.

'Actually, about that...'

'Yes?'

Michael could practically hear Jamie sitting up in bed, probably giving his wife a look.

'When you met Kelly...'

'Hmm?'

'Did you, erm, ever...dream about her?' Michael rushed the last few words, screwing his eyes shut and keeping his voice low.

There was a long pause over the phone.

'Jamie?'

'I'm here. No, I don't think so. What do you mean? Why do you ask? Who are you dreaming about?'

A smile touched Michael's lips.

'Which question should I answer first?'

'The last one,' said Jamie after some thought.

Michael had been afraid of that.

'The woman who bought the farmhouse.'

There was another pause, sharper this time.

'The one I double-dared you to ask out?'

'Yeah. And Mum's now added to that, she's triple-dared me. Sometimes I wonder where you get it from.'

'Ha! Triple dare, Mike. You've got to do it. And now you're dreaming about this woman?'

'Hmm.'

'What sort of dreams?' There was no disguising the smirk on Jamie's face coming through his voice.

'Exactly what you're thinking,' Michael mumbled.

'Oh, Mikey! For the love of everything, ask the woman out. Do you know her name yet?'

'Yes.'

'Then ask her. Was there anything else?'

'So, you never dreamt about Kelly?'

'Not before I asked her out, no.'

'Okay.'

'Why? It's not difficult to understand. You met her, she's beautiful, you want her, you're dreaming about her. Your brain and your body are both telling you to ask the woman out. What's the worst that could happen?'

'She laughs in my face,' Michael grumbled.

'And then you'll know you dodged a bullet. What's the best that can happen? I'll tell you the best that can happen. You fall in love and you get to live in that farmhouse. Win-win. Ask her out. Remember, there's a triple dare on you now. Is that everything?'

'Yes. Thanks, I guess.'

'G'night, brother.'

'Good night.'

Michael stared at his phone as Jamie managed to hang up first.

When they were children, Jamie had often dared him to do things. To throw a rock at a wall or skate down a steep road or throw a snowball at the boy who bullied him (he'd flat out refused that one, so Jamie had thrown the snowball, gotten into a fight with the boy and they'd both been suspended from school for two weeks. Michael still felt guilty about it).

Still staring at his phone, Michael considered his brother's words, trying to keep the memories of last night's dream at bay. What really was the worst that could happen if he just asked Frankie out for a drink next time he saw her?

Taking a deep breath, Michael vowed to do just that. Then he stopped.

'Oh, damn,' he murmured, waking up his phone and bringing up his messages.

Hi. Not sure I can do that date anymore.

He hit send and went to put his phone down when the three dots appeared. He waited for Dane

124

to reply.

What?! No no no. It's arranged. It's sorted. What's wrong? Are you not well? Come on, mate. What's the worst that could happen?

Michael stared at that last question long and hard. In a logical sense, it could perhaps be silly to cancel a date when he hadn't attempted to ask out Frankie yet. If she did say no, a dinner with another woman might be a good distraction.

Pulling a face, Michael forced himself to type out a reply.

Ok. I guess you're right. See you then.

Michael unstuck his tongue from the roof of his mouth and then jumped hard, his heart landing in his throat, as the practice's head receptionist knocked on his door.

'Your one o'clock is here,' she said kindly.

'Thank you.'

She closed the door, leaving Michael alone again, to calm his pounding heart and slow his breathing. He checked the time and went to stand, pausing to sigh. He'd forgotten to eat lunch. Again.

Thirteen

If Frankie forgot just how many rooms the farm-house had, she could almost relax. Builders were arriving the next day to start knocking down the wall between the old kitchen and dining room, and start on the small extension on the back. In the meantime, she'd taken out the downstairs bath-room successfully on her own and ripped up most of the threadbare carpets. Original floorboards had been waiting underneath, covered in dust and grime. Frankie had immediately hired a sander and done her best to resist taking her sledgehammer to the upstairs bathroom. Smashing out a sink that refused to move was incredibly therapeutic, but if she took out her impatience upstairs, she'd have nowhere to wash.

One step at a time, she reminded herself.

When she'd bought the doer-upper in London, shortly after quitting her acting career, she'd hired the builders and let them get on with it while she lived in a one-bed flat she'd bought exactly for that purpose. Keenly aware of how lucky she was,

Frankie had spent a year donating part of her money to good causes while trying to figure out what she wanted to do with the rest of her life as the builders did their thing. She'd moved into that house, ready to finish off the flooring, tiling and decorating herself as soon as the builders were finished and out. Now, she wasn't sure what working alongside builders in her home would be like. Not having a kitchen meant she could at least spend a lot of time in her parents' kitchen, brewing cups of tea and popping to the local shop for cake, rather than be in the way. But there were other rooms she could be working on while they took down walls and built new ones.

Wringing her hands at the thought, Frankie wandered into the second bedroom to find Lee, the local tradesman she'd hired, plastering the walls.

'Oh, it looks so different!' she exclaimed, and then apologised for making him jump. He gave her a smile and went back to work.

'This room'll be done today. I'll get started on the next room tomorrow.'

'Amazing. Thank you.'

'Should be done in a couple of days, then just let me know when downstairs is ready to go.'

Frankie nodded.

'Great. Thanks.'

Lee was her age with tattoos sprawling down his arms, visible only because he'd pushed the sleeves of his jumper up. Frankie's mother had given her daughter a wide-eyed look when he'd knocked on the door a couple of days before, ready to start re-plastering the rooms that didn't need any major work. Frankie had admonished her mother at the time, but it was hard not to notice what Irene had noticed.

Lee wasn't exactly unattractive.

His short blond hair extended to a short beard, framing dazzling blue eyes and soft lips that gave way to a gentle Edinburgh accent. He'd grown up around here, apparently. Frankie had found it hard not to quiz him over the first cup of tea she'd brought him.

She gazed over him now and found herself having the sort of thoughts she couldn't tell anyone else about. She immediately shut those down. Poor Lee, coming into the workplace to be gawped at. Instead, she turned her attention to his plastering.

'I always wanted to learn to plaster,' she mur-mured. 'Probably should have tried it a couple of years ago, when I was renovating my first house. It's a tricky skill to learn, isn't it?'

'There's a knack to it,' said Lee.

'I did all the tiling in my last house,' said Frankie, mostly for something to say, although she partly wondered if he'd be impressed. She'd always been bad at this sort of thing.

'My wife enjoys tiling.'

The air rushed out of Frankie. She bit her lip to stop herself from swearing under her breath.

'Oh, that's nice. Do you ever get to work together?'

'Oh no. She's a manager for a big company in the city. But I guess we redid our kitchen together. I plastered the walls, she tiled them.' Lee smiled to himself. 'Did a good job, too. She learned it all online.'

'Hmm. Me too.'

'Amazing what you can learn online these days, isn't it. Good thing plastering's hard, or I might be out of a job.'

Frankie gave a small laugh and then stopped when Lee looked at her.

'Do you want to give it a go?' he asked eventually.

There was a beat as Frankie stared at him.

'Really? I mean, isn't that just more work for you?'

Lee laughed and Frankie relaxed a little.

'True.'

'Plus, I'll slow you down,' Frankie added, staring up at the walls he'd already replastered.

'If you're anything like my missus, you'll be trying it yourself anyway, soon as I'm gone. I could give you some pointers, at least. Here.' He offered her the trowel and gestured to the bucket of plaster at his feet. 'Try it on this bit. Scoop up some plaster, slap it on the wall and then it's all in the wrist action.'

His eyes flashed and Frankie hesitated, unsure of what to make of that. Still, she did as she was told, scooping up the plaster from the bucket, placing it against the wall as she'd seen him do, and attempting to glide it over the wall. The trowel wouldn't glide and she skipped over a bump, almost dropping it. Plaster dropped to the floor and Frankie whistled.

'I see what you mean about wrist action.'

Again, Lee laughed, a gentle noise that Frankie could imagine his wife had immediately become smitten with.

'Here.' Lee tidied up around her, scooped up more plaster and placed it on the wall. 'Try again. Like this.' He mimicked the movement and, taking the trowel, she tried to copy him. The plaster went on easier, although a little thick, and she began to work to thin it and make it even.

'This would take me years!' Frankie grinned. 'Fun, though. Thanks, but I think I did the right thing hiring a professional.'

She did her best not to watch his arms as he took over from her.

'I guess you won't have this place ready for Christmas,' he said, breaking her thoughts.

'No. I might still put up some decorations, though. Seems a shame to not have some fairy lights up. Especially outside.'

'Absolutely.'

'Did you ever see this place when the previous owners lived here?'

'Nope. But I know what I'd do, if this was mine.'

'Oh? What's that?' Frankie smiled, always open to ideas.

'Lights all along the front of the house and one of those projectors. Maybe some fake snow. My little girl would love that.'

Little girl! This just got better and better. Frankie's gaze fell from his tattoos and she sighed through her nose.

'That sounds good,' she said. 'Make a real feature of the front.'

'It's a good-looking house.'

'Yeah. I was thinking of getting an oak porch made,' Frankie let slip. She snapped her mouth shut as Lee blew out a whistle.

'Nice. That would look good with lights.'

Frankie grinned.

'It would, wouldn't it? I'll have to get some lights, but I don't want to get in the builders' way, so it might have to wait until Christmas week.'

Lee shrugged as he worked.

'Better than never.'

There was a pause as Frankie considered this, glancing behind her, out of the window to the gravelled driveway beneath them. Frowning, she turned a little and then moved to the window. She was too late to see her mother, but she heard the front door open with a bang, and then, 'Frankie!'

Heart stopping, chest aching, Frankie was out of the room and flying down the stairs to her mother.

'What? What's wrong?'

'Lily!' cried Irene, pointing back out the open front door. 'She's eaten something in the garden and won't stop drooling. She's all wobbly.'

Frankie froze on the stairs, her heart pounding so hard it was deafening. Then she leapt down the last few steps and pulled out her phone.

'Do you know what she ate?'

'I...I think so.'

'Grab some of it. Where's Lily?'

Irene turned and Frankie followed her gaze, spotting the cocker spaniel in the cottage's front doorway, her head down, drool dripping from her jaws, tail between her legs, her back hunched as she swayed.

'Let's get her in the car. Lee!' Frankie turned back to the stairs to find the plasterer at the top looking down to her. 'Will you be okay on your own?'

'Of course. Get the dog to the vets.'

'I'll be in touch if we're long,' Frankie cried, grabbing her keys and finding the veterinary practice's phone number as she closed the door behind her and ran for the car. She opened the doors as the phone rang and then rushed to Lily's side.

'Sandy! It's Frankie. Lily's eaten something and now she's not well, drooling and looking really bad. Maybe she's eaten something toxic?'

'Bring her in right now, I'll let Michael know.'

Frankie barely registered the mention of Michael.

'On our way,' she almost shouted, hanging up the phone and approaching the dog. Lily attempted to wag her tail as she began panting. 'Okay, baby girl. Everything's going to be okay. Come on.' Gently, Frankie put her arms around Lily and lifted the dog, moving as quickly as she could towards the car. Lily was placed in her bed and the door closed just as Irene reappeared.

'Where's Dad?' Frankie asked, moving to the driver's seat and beckoning for her mother to get in the passenger side.

'At the shops. I'll call him.'

Frankie started the ignition and was pulling out of the driveway when she glanced at the torn-up plant in Irene's lap. If anything happened to Lily, it would be her fault. This was her house, her land, she should have checked the garden for toxic plants.

'Lily doesn't normally eat plants, does she?' she asked breathlessly, her chest still aching.

'It was in the long grass. An old bit of daffodil attached to a bulb. She's eaten the bulb. We should have checked it.' Irene's voice was tight and she turned back to look at the dog, reaching out a hand to stroke Lily's ear. 'I'm so sorry, my sweet girl. You hang on in there. We'll get you feeling better.'

Frankie put her foot down, cursing the speed limit, as they rushed into town, hoping against hope that there would be a parking spot outside the vets.

Fourteen

Michael was ready and waiting when Frankie, her mother and Lily the dog arrived. Sandy had managed to secure a parking spot outside the front of the practice by standing in it after she'd made Michael aware of the situation. Michael stepped outside to lift the dog up and carry her into the practice. Frankie and her mother followed, her mother telling Michael what had happened and showing him the plant.

'She was eating the long grass – we haven't had a chance to mow it yet – and there are daffodil bulbs in there. She's never showed any interest in daffodils or bulbs before, but she pulled it up when she was eating the grass and she'd swallowed the bulb before I could stop her. It was only small. She probably barely noticed it. But then she started drooling and swaying and, and, and...'

'It's all right,' said Michael, trying to keep his tone gentle as he placed Lily on the floor and watched her carefully. He bent to check her eyes and inside her mouth, rubbing around her belly as Lily gave a gentle moan. 'We'll induce vomiting. I've already prepared it, it's just a quick injection.' He picked up the syringe he'd prepared, using Lily's notes from the previous week, and bent down next to the door, whispering to her. Lily attempted a tail wag and flinched as the needle went into her scruff.

'My poor baby. I'm so sorry.' Irene sat on a chair Sandy had brought in and Lily moved to rest her chin on Irene's lap.

Frankie kneeled and stroked the dog as Lily snuffled at her. Michael's eyes were locked on Lily, watching her for any sign of something awful about to happen.

'I'll bring in something to catch the sick,' came Sandy's voice, and she returned a moment later with absorbent puppy pads, which she laid on the floor ready to catch any vomit.

'Come on, Lil. Bring it up,' said Frankie gently.

Michael leaned back against the consultation table and sighed softly through his nose. Come on, Lily.

Licking repeatedly, Lily stopped and arched her back.

'Here we go,' murmured Michael.

Lily put down her head, opened her mouth and vomited up a pile of partly digested food, long grass and there, in the middle of the pile, a small daffodil bulb.

'Good girl!' cried Irene, rubbing the dog's

shoulder.

'Well done, Lil,' said Frankie.

Michael allowed himself one quick glance at the woman he was beginning to feel was haunting his dreams. Her large eyes were red rimmed and filled with unspent tears. She wiped at them with the back of her hand and, glancing up to find her mother crying, she reached to take Irene's hand.

Michael bit on his lip and turned his attention back to the dog. Sandy removed the vomit and replaced the puppy pads before Michael could think to move. She scooped up the pad containing the vomit and placed it on the table beside him.

'One small daffodil bulb,' he said. 'Do you know for certain that's all she ate?' He used a pen to leaf through the greenery in the vomit. There was long grass and some brown scraps of old daffodil leaves.

'Yes. Just one small one. I saw it. I know I did. Been replaying it in my head over and over all the way here.'

'Right, well, I might give her some charcoal, just to soak up any other toxins. And maybe some fluids, see if we can flush it all out,' Michael mused, partly to himself, as he watched Lily.

She was already starting to look brighter, although her eyes had gone sleepy from the medication. The dog leaned into Irene as she gave Lily a cuddle.

'Yes, I'll give her some charcoal and then I think she can go home and sleep it off.' He glanced up at

Irene. 'You might want to check the rest for the garden for hidden bulbs.'

Irene nodded emphatically.

'The moment we get home and she's settled.'

'I'll help,' said Frankie, who was now sitting on the floor. She didn't look up at Michael, her gaze firmly fixed on the dog.

Michael left the room, taking the vomit-filled pads with him. He disposed of the vomit and offending bulb, and thanked Sandy for her help, then he wandered into the room where the medicines were kept and took a moment. Leaning his palms flat on the worktop, he closed his eyes and took a breath.

'Are you all right?'

Michael jumped, his eyes flying open, and Sandy held up her hands.

'Sorry. Sorry, I didn't mean to scare you. A strong cup of tea? I'll offer the ladies tea, too. I think they could do with something warm.'

'Yes. Good idea. Thank you, Sandy.'

Michael watched the now empty space Sandy had occupied, his mind whirring.

When he ventured out of the room, pushing back the thoughts of Frankie and the triple dare being held against him, he found Frankie, her mother and Lily still in the consultation room, sipping cups of hot tea. He gave Lily a dose of activated charcoal, which she happily lapped up, and then offered them refuge in the consultation room for a little while. Again, he escaped, but this time out into the waiting room where Sandy was sitting at the reception desk.

'Hate these things,' said Sandy. 'Not the sort of adrenaline you want.'

'Absolutely,' Michael agreed, glancing back to the consultation room.

Sandy stood.

'I was about to get the Christmas decs when they called. Do you think I can carry on with that? The dog's okay, isn't she?'

Michael nodded distractedly.

'Oh yes, Lily should be fine. You go ahead.' He took a moment to watch Sandy as she reached for the box containing the practice's old Christmas tree hidden under her desk, trying desperately to remember what he wanted to ask her. 'You did brilliantly,' he started.

Sandy beamed.

'Thank you. I know you could have handled that yourself, I hope I didn't impose.'

'No. Absolutely not.'

'I know it's more the job of the nurses.'

Michael wrung his hands, glancing back into the practice where the other vet on duty was chatting to a couple of nurses about an upcoming surgery. Sandy pulled out the box and opened it, revealing the tree that had been bought by the practice's previous owners.

'Oh. Do we need a new tree?' Michael put a hand

through his hair. 'How do we get a new tree? That one's very shabby.'

'I heard about a company near the city that rents out potted ones.'

'Perfect,' said Michael. 'Look into that and find out how much it costs. Much better than that old thing, although we could put it up in the meantime, maybe?'

Sandy nodded.

'It can go in the staff room when we get the other tree. Like a semi-retirement.' She chuckled to herself and began to battle with the plastic tree in a bid to assemble it. Michael stepped forward to help.

'I'm going to be hiring at least one head vet,' Michael said, unsure of where to start and so letting the words just fall out.

'Oh?'

'Yes. For this practice or my city one. Or maybe a head vet for each, I'm not sure yet.'

'Is this so you can take more of a back seat?' Sandy asked as the tree clicked into place and they both stood back to look at it.

'In theory,' said Michael. 'Things can't carry on the way they are.'

'Well, it's not my place to say, I know, but no, they can't,' said Sandy, offering him a smile.

'It hasn't escaped my notice that you pretty much run this place single-handedly,' Michael continued, glancing up to see if any of his other employees were listening. There were only the two nurses in that day and they had vanished along with the vet.

'Well, thank you,' said Sandy, breaking into his thoughts. 'That's why you gave me that very appreciated pay rise when you bought the place. And I really am grateful for that, and for you keeping me on. I do love this job, you know.'

'I know.' Michael gave Sandy the warmest smile he could muster. 'Which is why I was wondering if you'd like a promotion?'

Sandy stared at him, her eyes widening a fraction.

'Meg is retiring soon. I wondered if you'd like the role of practice manager?'

Sandy went to gasp but sucked it back in and snapped her mouth shut. Then her eyes narrowed.

'Would that mean more paperwork and office stuff, and less talking to the clients and their animals?'

Michael almost laughed.

'Probably,' he admitted. 'But you could make the role your own. You know I'm happy as long as the work gets done. You'd be in charge of those on reception, rotas, running the practice as a whole. We already have someone to do the admin and finance, so it's not that much paperwork. What do you think?'

'I—'

'And a pay rise to go with it, of course.'

Sandy, her mouth still open from when Michael

had interrupted, stared at him.

He was about to say something, to nudge her back to reality, when Frankie's voice from behind made him jump, his heart leaping into his throat. He turned to find Frankie looking around him to the tree, two empty cups in her hand.

'Sorry. I didn't mean to interrupt. I just...' Finally, she looked up into Michael's eyes. He froze. 'I just wanted to say thank you. Really, a massive thank you. For all of that. It was a genuine mistake and I don't know what we'd do if something happened to Lily.'

Michael urged himself to speak, but his mouth and vocal cords refused.

'Oh, that's all right,' said Sandy. 'It happens a lot. You wouldn't believe. Especially this time of year. Dogs and cats eating mistletoe and holly and chocolate and mince pies. One dog last year got into the freshly baked stash of mince pies and chocolate brownies and scarfed the lot.'

'Oh no! Were they all right?'

'Oh, yes. And probably a little too pleased with themselves.' Sandy laughed, jolting Michael back to the room. 'The owners weren't happy. They'd spent all day baking and poof! It was all gone in a matter of minutes. If you have a Labrador, keep them out of the kitchen at Christmas.' Sandy grinned.

'That makes me feel better.'

'It happens in summer, too. This summer we had a Doberman that munched her way through her owner's compost heap.'

Michael made them both jump by laughing.

'That was a fun one. Once we knew she was okay, of course. She threw up all sorts, including a sock.'

'Who puts a sock in the compost?' Sandy laughed, ducking suddenly and reappearing with a box of baubles and tinsel.

Michael glanced down, wondering what else was hidden beneath her desk.

'How is Lily doing?' he asked Frankie.

Frankie nodded.

'She's back to her normal self, I think. Just a little tired and wobbly.'

'Yes, she'll need to sleep it off. She should be back to being Lily tomorrow.'

'Mum's just called my dad, I assume he's already out in the garden digging it all up.'

'There's no one to blame,' said Michael. 'These things happen. And you did the right thing, bringing her in immediately.'

'Thank you.' Frankie slowly met Michael's eyes and there was a silence that seemed to go on for too long, but, at the same time, Michael didn't want it to end. Now was the time, he realised. All he had to do was ask if she wanted to go for a drink sometime.

He cleared his throat.

But how could he? She'd just had the fright of her life. Her mother was still in the consultation room, probably dabbing up spent tears and cuddling her dog. Frankie was having to take care of all of it, and she still had to drive them home.

No, now wasn't the time. But he'd cleared his throat and now Frankie was looking at him expectantly.

'Keep an eye on her, and if anything happens, you're worried or she starts acting strangely, just give us a call.'

Was it his imagination or did Frankie deflate a little? She covered it with a nod.

'Thank you. What if it happens after hours? Do you have an emergency line?'

'No. We don't run an out-of-hours line, but there's another practice a few towns over that's a twenty-four-hour hospital. I'll find you their number,' said Sandy, returning to her desk.

'If you need anything out of hours, give me a call,' Michael found himself saying. He reached back to Sandy's desk and grabbed a Post-it note and pen, scribbled down his number and gave it to Frankie. 'Anytime,' he added, his gaze flicking back up to hers.

She took it and gave a slow, sweet smile that twisted Michael's stomach into knots.

'Thanks. Should we stay or can we get out of your way?' Frankie asked, glancing up as a woman with a cat carrier walked through the front door. Sandy greeted the woman, leaving the Christmas tree and decorations behind.

'You're free to go when you're ready,' Michael told Frankie.

Frankie thanked him again, waved his number at him with another smile, and then disappeared back into the consultation room. Michael watched her go, his legs weakening, his throat dry, fighting a desperate urge to follow her.

'Michael?' Sandy's voice came through and Michael mentally shook himself.

'Hmm?'

'Erm, your two o'clock is here.' Sandy gestured at the smiling woman with the cat.

'Of course. Mrs Eames and Maestro. Give me five minutes and I'll be right with you. Please, take a seat.' Michael gave Sandy a nod. 'Let me know what you think about the job proposal,' he added quietly.

Sandy grinned.

'I can let you know now. Yes, please!'

Frankie, Irene and Lily emerged from the consultation room and Irene thanked both Michael and Sandy, her cheeks stained red with tears. Michael waved them off and then returned to the consultation room to give it a clean and start his afternoon of appointments, unable to wipe the smile from his face.

Fifteen

A week passed without hiccup or occasion. Lily recovered quickly and was back to her normal self a day later, but she slept through Geoff and Frankie digging up every bulb they could find in the garden. Everything was cut back, even the grass, despite the cold, damp weather.

Exhausted, Frankie's parents had shut the curtains on their cottage to rest for a day, while Frankie turned her attention back to her farmhouse and the arrival of the builders. The Post-it note with Michael's number should have gone on her parents' fridge, in case of an emergency, but for some reason Frankie had stuck it to the wall of her bedroom, out of sight of the builders but within easy reach.

She glanced at it every night as she climbed into bed, replaying the moment Michael's eyes had lit up and he'd calmly told her to call him instead of an emergency veterinary hospital. She was sure Sandy had told her he lived in the city. What good would he be, she wondered, in an emergency when he was so far away?

Every morning that week, she searched for the Post-it when she opened her eyes and would stare at that square with his scribbled handwriting until she found the will to climb out of bed.

The farmhouse was cold. The heating system was ancient and juddery, and the new boiler and heating system wasn't being installed until the right walls had been knocked down, giving the plumber access. For now, the chill December crept in through the cracks around the windows that would likely need replacing and beneath the door that was original and absolutely not being touched.

That morning, Frankie dressed and stood staring at the window. It had been an internal argument, trying to figure out what should be done first and what should follow. She knew the windows needed replacing, but for some reason had decided that they could wait until the building work was complete. She'd almost forgotten about the Scottish winter.

The builders arrived brisk and early, so Frankie arranged the tea mugs and tea bags, along with a plate of biscuits and box of donuts she'd bought the evening before, and left them to it. She escaped to her parents' cottage – their lovely, warm cottage – to defrost, eat a bacon roll her father had prepared and discuss the plans for the day.

Geoff was still having trouble letting Lily out of his sight, so once his bacon roll was devoured, he clipped on her lead and set about a morning walk.

'How was book club last night?' Frankie asked as the front door shut behind her father and Lily.

'It was fun.' Irene didn't look up and Frankie narrowed her eyes.

'Did something happen?'

'What? No.'

'You're not telling me something.'

'Okay, but you have to promise not to laugh, judge or try and stop me from going back.'

'Oh, Mum! What on earth happened at book club?' Frankie gave a nervous smirk and tried to cover it up by bringing her coffee cup to her lips. 'It can't have been that different to when I went with you?'

'Oh... Well...'

'Well?'

'Well, you remember how when you came, we all talked about the book and a couple of the ladies hadn't read it, so we ended up just talking about life and Edinburgh?'

'Hmm? Had you all read the book this time?'

'No.'

Frankie waited and then groaned.

'Mum! Come on, tell me. Please? It can't be worse than the stories I'm making up while you don't tell me.'

Irene laughed.

'Fine. This time we discussed some problems we were having, and...'

'And?'

'Solutions to those problems.'

Frankie frowned.

'Okay. I don't understand why you couldn't tell me that? So you're a group of older women who support one another? That's lovely.'

'With some witchcraft,' said Irene, taking a gulp of her coffee.

Frankie stared at her.

'Excuse me?'

'Well, you see, Esme – isn't she lovely? – it turns out her youngest son is a bit lonely, so they did something of a love spell. This was before I joined them, obviously. But apparently it isn't working. So last night we...did another one. He has a date coming up this week and she wanted to give him an extra boost.'

Frankie blinked a few times, wondering how to react. At first, she fought back the smile, then changed her mind and laughed.

'Okay. I thought love spells didn't exist? Or is that just genie wishes? You can't make someone fall in love.'

Irene shrugged.

'It's not that kind of love spell, though, is it.'

'I don't know, Mum. You're the expert.'

Irene shot her daughter a look and Frankie hid a scoff behind another gulp of coffee.

'It's a spell that encourages love to enter his life. We weren't asking him to fall in love with a specific person, or for them to fall in love with him. We were only asking the Universe to bring that right person into his life.'

Frankie gave this some thought, her smile fading a little.

'Maybe I could use some of that,' she murmured.

Irene patted her daughter's hand.

'I thought you'd given up on men.'

'Oh, pfft. Like I meant that. We're in Scotland! Where there are gorgeous, sexy Scottish accents. Who moves to Scotland to be done with men?'

Irene smiled at Frankie.

'Well, maybe you were sending the Universe the wrong message.'

Frankie studied her mother.

'This book club has changed you.'

Irene laughed.

'Are you still going to come into the city with me this morning? We'd best get going, otherwise I'll be late for my painting class, and today we're doing life drawing.'

'Ooh, male or female?'

'I don't know. If it's a handsome, well-endowed man, shall I give him your number?'

Frankie laughed but didn't say no. Instead, her mind went back to the Post-it note on her bedroom wall. She'd have to pop in to tell Sandy how Lily was doing, and if Michael happened to be there too, then so be it.

The wind was howling through Edinburgh, but that didn't bother Frankie. She held on to her mother tightly before leaving her at her painting class and venturing back out into New Town. Pulling her hat tight around her ears, for fear of it being blown off, she marched as best she could to Queen Street and reached the road just as drops of rain began to fall. It shouldn't last long, she decided, given the strength of the wind. Looking up, she realised how wrong she was. The sky was a solid dark grey of clouds filled with rain, there was no end in sight. Puffing out her cheeks, Frankie strode on down the road as the wind lashed raindrops at her face, her eyes beginning to sting and her lips going numb with the cold. Soon the gardens to her left ended, to be replaced with tall, elegant red-bricked buildings. On her right was an equally red but much more dazzling building. If it wasn't for the rain and wind, Frankie would have paused to gaze up at the carvings of people decorating small turrets at the corners of the vast building. Instead, she pulled her hat lower, put her head down and jogged to the main entrance of the National Portrait Gallery.

There was one reason Frankie visited the Scottish National Portrait Gallery, and only one reason: the beautifully painted ceiling in the main hall. And the café. So, two reasons.

She'd discovered the gallery on a much wetter day many years ago, when visiting Edinburgh with her mother. They'd gotten caught on Queen Street as the rain began to fall in sheets, had looked up at the carved masterpieces and sought shelter inside the building they hadn't known existed. That had been the first time Frankie had seen that ceiling in the main hall, now made famous by tourism influencers on social media. It had also been the first time she'd discovered the scones in the café.

Just inside the main entrance was a small but elegant tree with twinkling lights. Frankie stopped to shake off the rain, and then slowly turned to watch the spitting droplets outside turn into pouring rain.

'Good timing,' said the security guard by the door.

Frankie agreed with a damp laugh, undid her coat and wandered through into the main hall. A Christmas tree stood in one corner and Frankie admired it for a moment, the twinkling fairy lights reflecting off the window beside the tree. Stepping further into the hall, she took a moment before looking up, savouring the chill of the stone walls and the ornate gold around the columns. The stained-glass windows in front of her, the archways, the stairs leading off to the galleries above, the inevitable smell of the cold, sandstone building that was two hundred years old. Frankie breathed in deep and then allowed herself to slowly look up.

The ceiling was a dark blue painted with stars and gold leaf in a square, sectioned off by other squares of the ceiling framework. Four lanterns hung down, giving off a dim, golden light that seemed more in keeping now that Christmas was approaching. Around the first-floor balustrade was a stunning frieze of famous Scots, showing off the history of the country. It was intricate and fascinating, but every time Frankie tried to study it, her eyes were drawn back up to that dark blue ceiling.

She could do something similar with her bed-room ceiling, she realised.

Checking there was no one around her – there were a few tourists reading the plaques around the hall and a couple bustled in from the rain but kept their distance as they started their own gradual gaze upwards – Frankie opened her arms, stared up at the ceiling and started to slowly twirl.

The dark blue and stars mingled, surrounding her, opening her chest and filling her with some-thing that made her want to laugh. Grinning, breathless, she stopped and glanced sheepishly around. A few people were smiling at her. She wrapped her coat around her once more, tucked her hair behind her ears and wandered over to the side, to allow for other twirlers, should they feel the need.

Once she'd caught her breath, Frankie left the main hall and disappeared through a corridor that led to the café and gallery shop. The café was decorated with fairy lights and tinsel, and a tall tree stood in one corner. A smile still playing on her lips, she moved over to the counter and surveyed what the café had on offer. A woman behind the counter watched patiently and smiled as Frankie looked up.

'Hi,' said Frankie.

'Good afternoon.'

'Can I get a latte and a cherry scone, please?'

'Of course. Butter and jam?'

'Yes, please.'

'You can choose your jam.' The woman gestured to a basket of little jam jars next to the scones as she chose the biggest cherry scone and placed it on a plate for Frankie. She entered it all on the till and, as Frankie paid, she turned away to make the coffee.

Frankie watched, vanishing a little into her own thoughts. She'd put a picture rail around the top of her bedroom walls and paint everything above it, including the ceiling, a dark blue. The rest of the walls would be white. Or perhaps something a little darker to make the room cosy. She'd have to wait and see. As she imagined how the room would eventually look, her mind showed her the Post-it note with Michael's number, stuck to the wall that might eventually be a bright white. Or maybe a soft blue-white.

The Post-it note wouldn't stay, of course. She'd have moved it long before she got around to decorating her bedroom. Maybe it would go on the brand-new fridge. For Lily's sake.

Her latte was placed on her tray and Frankie thanked the woman, turning to find a table. She chose a small table in the corner, out of the way, where she could watch the comings and goings, while also being close enough to the window to watch the rain. Getting comfortable, her back to the wall, she glanced up and her heart jolted, her eyes meeting Michael's.

It couldn't be him.

She had to be seeing things.

She blinked, barely breathing, and Michael turned away, looking anywhere else but at her. He was sitting at a table near the middle of the café, facing a woman with silver hair tied up in a bun. Frankie blinked again, wondering who the woman reminded her of.

Again, her heart jolted as the woman glanced awkwardly over her shoulder, met Frankie's eyes and gave a little wave.

Little pieces started to fall together as Frankie attempted a smile and waved back to Esme.

Sixteen

Michael was running late. He knew it wasn't a problem, his mother was used to him running late, it was more that every time they met, he promised he wouldn't be late. The rain was falling heavily as he reached the National Portrait Gallery and he swore under his breath. If he'd been on time, he wouldn't have gotten wet. There was no one to blame but himself. Unless he blamed the paperwork he'd gotten lost in back at the city practice. It wasn't even work he could delegate. His father had been wise enough to hire an office manager for the practice's main admin and Michael hadn't dared touch any of his father's systems. Still, he wondered how his father had really coped.

He'd only had the one practice and wasn't working for a charity on top of it all, Michael reminded himself. He smiled and nodded at the security guard on his way into the gallery, quickly shaking off the rain before he entered the main hall. There'd be no time to look up. His mother would be waiting for him in the café.

Michael came to a juddering halt and blinked hard, even going so far as to rub his eyes. He had to be seeing things. The woman standing in the middle of the main hall, twirling while looking up at the ceiling couldn't possibly be Frankie. He took a shuddering breath, watching her long, dark hair fan out behind her, her arms outstretched, damp coat open to show off a long, multi-coloured dress beneath. She wore a green beanie hat on her head but didn't seem that wet. How long had she been here?

Realising he was still late and that Frankie might stop at any moment and turn to him, or worse yet, turn out to not be Frankie, Michael ripped his gaze away and strode down the corridor towards the café and shop.

'I'm sorry, I'm sorry.'

'It's okay, my love,' said Esme. 'I've been here an hour reading the paper.' She gestured to her empty pot of tea. 'I knew something would probably come up. The animals always come first.'

Michael gave a guilty sigh and then ventured to the woman behind the counter, ordering a couple of coffees and two scones: one fruit and one cherry.

'I hope there wasn't an emergency?' his mother asked as he brought it all over to the table. 'You're allowed to cancel, you know. If something comes up.'

'No, no. I just got lost in paperwork,' said Michael, peeling off his wet coat. 'Completely my

156

own fault. My city practice could use a Sandy, if I'm honest.'

'A Sandy?'

'Hmm. She's the receptionist who came with the rural practice. She's a godsend. She'd have knocked on my door and reminded me I was going to be late well before I could be late. I sort of wish I could clone her.'

Esme laughed.

'Speaking of employees, are you creating new positions?'

Michael nodded.

'We're going to be recruiting at least one head vet—'

'You should hire two,' Esme interjected.

'—and promoting Sandy to practice manager.'

'Ooh, practice manager.'

'Yes, when Meg retires. She's the practice manager who came with the rural practice.'

'And yet you're still doing all that paperwork.' Esme tutted.

'I haven't changed anything about the city practice, it's all as Dad had it. I'm not sure how he managed.'

'He did rather like doing everything himself,' mused Esme. 'A tad of a control freak. Let's face it, Michael, you don't take after me much. Which, while I love you, I was always a little annoyed about. Do you know how long I was in labour with you?'

'Twelve hours,' Michael recited.

'And you tore me.'

'Mum!'

Esme gave a soft cackle and then stopped as she looked up at her youngest son.

'What's wrong?'

'Nothing.' Michael averted his gaze from Frankie, paying for her coffee and scone. He studied his own scone carefully.

'No, come on. What is it?' Esme asked. She glanced around and saw the back of Frankie's head. 'Oh, do you know her?' Esme turned back to Michael with a smile that made his stomach lurch.

'She's the woman who bought the farmhouse in BekBurn,' he murmured. 'Don't say anything,' he added.

Esme gave him a strange look.

'I met her a while ago. I forgot to mention it to you.'

'What?' Michael straightened, almost forgetting that Frankie was right behind his mother, heading for a table in the corner.

'Yes. It turns out the newcomer to the book club is her mother. Irene. She's lovely. And so is Frankie.'

'You know her name?'

'Yes, don't you?'

'Yes. Her and her mother rushed their dog into the practice a week ago. She ate a daffodil bulb.'

'Oh no! Irene didn't mention that. Is she all

right?'

Michael nodded distractedly.

'Of course. We looked after her.'

'Good boy.'

'Frankie went to the book club, too?'

'Well, she dropped her mother off and she'd found a good parking space. It would have been a shame to let her lose it and rude to not invite her in. She hasn't joined the book club, though. Her mother has.' Esme smiled to herself, studying her son.

Michael didn't notice. Frankie had taken a seat with her back to the wall, facing the café, and as she glanced around, their eyes met for one tantalising moment. Without meaning to, Michael looked away and found himself suddenly fascinated by the top of the table between him and his mother.

'She's the one your brother's dared you to ask out, isn't she? Do you fancy her?' Esme whispered.

Then, to Michael's horror, Esme turned awkwardly in her seat, found Frankie and waved.

Blood rushed up to Michael's face and he looked up in time to see Frankie smile and wave back. What if she came over? What if his mother invited her to join them? Michael's throat tightened.

'Well? Do you?' Esme turned back to her son, buttering her scone.

'Mum. Do we have to?'

'We don't have to, but I would like to,' said Esme, matter-of-factly. 'Come on. Indulge your poor, old mother.'

Michael sighed, looking down. If he avoided his mother's eyes, he couldn't see Frankie sitting behind her.

'There's nothing to indulge,' he said. 'Nothing to tell. She bought the old farmhouse in Bekburn—'

'Yes, I know.'

'—And last week her parents' dog was sick—'

'You said.'

'—And yes, Jamie dared me, but I could hardly ask her out when she was in shock about her poor dog.'

'Of course.'

'—And that's all there is to it.'

Esme studied her son and Michael swallowed a little too hard.

'And have you done a follow up?' she asked, leaning forward to take a bite out of her buttered scone.

'What?'

'For the dog,' said Esme with her mouth full.

'Oh. Yes, of course. I spoke to Frankie's mother.'

'Irene.' Esme swallowed. 'Her mother's name is Irene.'

Michael sighed and stared at his mother, doing his best to ignore the blurred vision of Frankie behind her.

'All of this is fine,' Esme continued. 'But none of it explains your current reaction. You've bumped into clients and women and ex-girlfriends before, you've never acted like this. Or gone that shade of red.'

Michael bit his tongue and looked back down to the table.

'There's something special about this woman, yet you don't seem to know much about her?'

Again, Michael sighed. He clenched his eyes shut, quickly weighing his options, and then he muttered, 'I've been dreaming about her.'

Esme's eyes widened, but only a little, and then she sipped her coffee and got herself under control.

'Oh? Since you met her?'

'Since before I met her.'

Esme spluttered and coughed, putting down her coffee with a shaking hand.

'Are you all right?' Michael was lifting out of his seat, wondering if she was choking, glancing around the café for assistance.

'I'm fine, I'm fine,' Esme croaked, finding a tissue in her pocket and waving him away. 'Wrong pipe, that's all. I'm fine.' She cleared her throat and wiped her mouth. 'You dreamt of her before you met her?' she checked, lowering her voice.

Michael nodded, and then his brow furrowed.

'Why? Why is that important?'

Esme shrugged and looked away.

'Mum. What are you not telling me?'

'Nothing. Nothing that would interest you.'

'Mum.'

'You're a man of science, Michael. You won't understand.'

'Just tell me. Please.'

Esme found another tissue and wiped some spots of spilled coffee from the table.

'My friends and I may have done a...spell...to help you...find someone.' She kept her gaze on the table and cleared her throat again.

Michael glared at her.

'What are you talking about? Which friends? What do you mean a spell?' he asked in a hushed voice.

'My...book club.'

Michael's eyes widened.

'We found a spell book in an old second-hand bookshop a long time ago, and sometimes, if one of us needs help with something, we'll give one of the spells a go.'

Michael relaxed a little. How much harm could a spell in a book do? He didn't even believe in any of that.

'You were so worried about me that you did a spell from a book?'

Esme nodded.

'I just want you to be happy, Michael. I want you to find someone. It's so wonderful that you're happy in work, that you've taken over your father's practice and expanded. And the charity work is even more wonderful. But there are other ways to be happy. Arguably more important ways. Do you think your father would have been as happy without me and you boys? No. Your line of work is hard, both physically and on the soul, and you need someone to go home to that isn't a cat. As much as I love Agnes. You need someone who will support you and hold you on the bad days. You need more love in your life to protect you from the grief and the horrors. I just wanted – I still want – you to find love.'

'Some people are very happy without finding a romantic partner,' Michael said slowly in a small voice.

Esme watched him and then leaned forward on the table.

'Do you want to be one of those people?'

Michael lifted his gaze to hers and automatically went to shake his head but stopped himself in time. His eyes flicked over her shoulder to Frankie, sipping her coffee and looking down at her phone.

'When did you do this spell of yours?' he asked gently.

'At the beginning of December.'

Michael's chest tightened.

'When did you first dream of her?' asked Esme, still leaning forward.

Michael met his mother's eyes and then looked away, back down to the table and his own untouched scone.

'Did the spell work?' Esme whispered. 'The Universe is pointing you towards her.'

'Oh, shh, Mum. It's not like that.'

Esme leaned back.

'How do you know?'

Michael took a deep breath and met his mother's eyes again.

'Look, I appreciate that you're worried about me. But you really shouldn't be. I'm happy. Everything is good and going well. Do I wish I could meet someone? Sure. Do I wish I could give you the grandchildren just down the road that you really want? Of course.'

'Michael,' Esme scolded quietly, but she went no further. He wasn't lying. She'd always tried to hide how much she missed her eldest child and the grandchildren she never got to see in person, but Michael had always been the person in their family who could see right through the act, into the depths of her.

'But life doesn't work that way. And I'm really sorry about that.' Michael paused, reaching out a hand to squeeze his mother's fingers. 'But I have you, and you have me.'

'That's not enough, Michael. It shouldn't be enough for you.'

'And I have a date coming up.'

'But not with Frankie?'

'Well, no.'

'Have you tried asking her out?'

'Only when she was busy looking after her mum who was fraught about almost losing their dog, and I couldn't. It would have been unprofessional and unethical. And I haven't seen her since.'

Esme gave this some thought.

'The café's quiet,' she murmured. 'You could go ask her now.'

Michael's heart leapt into his throat and he snatched his hand back.

'I—'

'Esme! Are you all right? I was worried you were choking earlier.'

Michael froze and looked up into the concerned face of Frankie, standing beside the table.

'Frankie! How lovely to bump into you. I'm perfectly fine, thank you. A bit of coffee going down the wrong way.'

'Oh, good. We've all been there!' Frankie gave a small laugh and then glanced at Michael. Mouth dry, Michael looked away, his mind racing.

'I understand you've met my son, Michael? He's your local vet, yes?'

'Yes, yes. He did an amazing job of helping my parents' dog when she ate something she shouldn't have. Thank you again.' Frankie gave Michael a beautiful smile and he could only give a singular nod in return.

'Frankie.' Esme grasped Frankie's hand and Michael's head almost exploded. 'I can't remember if you mentioned when you came to book club – are you single?'

Frankie did a short, nervous laugh.

'It usually depends on who's asking,' she said. 'But as it's you, yes, I am.' She glanced at Michael again, almost so quickly it could have been imagined, and then her attention was back on Esme.

'Wonderful. So is Michael.' Esme let that hang in the air for a moment as both Frankie and Michael stared at her.

'Oh,' said Frankie, when the silence became too much. 'That's nice.' She met Michael's eyes and opened her mouth to say more when the phone in her pocket began ringing. The sound echoed around the café and Frankie jumped, grabbing at it to make it quiet. 'Sorry! Sorry. That's my mum. She's at a painting class doing, erm, what's it called? When you draw naked people.'

'Life drawing? I've always wanted to try that.' Esme's eyes brightened.

'You should ask her about it at the next book club,' said Frankie quickly.

'I certainly will.'

'I'd best take this, make sure she's okay.' Frankie gave Michael another look. 'Nice to see you both.'

'Take care in the rain!' Esme called after her as Frankie strode from the café, her phone to her ear. 'Why didn't you ask for her number or something?' she hissed at her son.

Michael put his face in his hands and groaned.

'Because her mum called?' he offered, picking up his knife and buttering his scone with more force than required. 'Can we just have our scones and coffee and talk about something else, please? What

166

would you like for Christmas?'

'Frankie as a daughter-in-law.'

Michael looked up at his mother and she gave a laugh.

'Sorry. Sorry. It would be nice, though.'

Glancing back over his shoulder, Michael searched the windows for any sign of Frankie. It would be nice, he thought, then he shook his head of such nonsense and took a big bite of his scone.

Seventeen

'Sorry I'm late, sorry I'm late! Ooh, is this for me?' Sandy appeared in the pub in a whirlwind of words and plonked into the chair opposite Frankie.

'Yes. Gin and tonic. You said you were having a bad day, so...' Frankie laughed. 'Is everything okay?'

'It's better than okay. Yes, I was having a bad day, which is why I said so this morning, but oh, Frankie! I'm so glad you suggested lunch today!'

Frankie waited, smiling, eyebrows raised, ready for some big important announcement.

'I,' said Sandy, full of importance, 'have just been officially promoted!' She gave a small scream and then downed half of the gin and tonic.

'Woah, take it easy. Unless you have the afternoon off?'

'I do not.'

'Promoted! Congratulations. What's the new role?'

'You're now looking at the new practice

manager! Meg, who's been practice manager practically since the place became a vets, has retired and Michael is promoting me, to give me more power and more money.'

At the mention of Michael's name, Frankie swallowed and sat back a little. Sandy didn't notice.

'That's fantastic. So, you're practice manager as of today?'

'Yes!' Sandy grinned and bounced in her seat. 'Although I have to cover reception still until he hires a new receptionist, but he wants me to help with that. I've never interviewed anyone, I've never been on the other side of that table. Have you?'

'No.'

'I can't wait! Let's order food, can't be late back.' Sandy gave another squeal and downed the last of her gin and tonic. 'That really hit the spot. Don't worry, I'll have lemonade from now on.'

They ordered their food and Frankie listened to Sandy explaining what her new role would mean for the practice and her savings account and her boyfriend's landscaping dreams while they waited for the food to arrive at their table.

'I'm so sorry. Enough about me and all my exciting news,' said Sandy, squirting out tomato sauce onto her chips. 'How are you? How's Lily doing? Is she okay?'

'Oh, more than okay. She's completely back to normal. Thank you again for all of that. I have no idea what we'd have done without you.'

'It's literally our jobs,' said Sandy, waving Frankie's words away and taking a bite of her fish finger sandwich.

'Yes, and you're very good at them. You and Michael. You really deserve that promotion. It's good of Michael to give you that extra power and money,' said Frankie carefully before taking a bite of her brie and cranberry sandwich.

'He's always been good. Such a good man.'

'I met his mother recently.'

Sandy stopped and stared at Frankie.

'Shut up! What's she like? Michael hardly ever mentions her but when I've talked to the receptionists at the city practice, they make her sound like some amazing goddess. She used to go in regularly to see Michael's dad, back when he owned the practice, and then to check on Michael.'

'She is amazing,' said Frankie. 'Really lovely. She runs a book club and my mum joined. Sort of serendipitous, in a weird way.'

Sandy gave her a strange look.

'How so?'

'Oh, you know, move to a new country and meet the local vet. Then go into the city to drop off my mum and get invited in by the said local vet's mother. It's weird, right?'

Sandy's smile had changed. Frankie wasn't sure what to make of it. She squirmed a little.

'Definitely weird,' Sandy agreed quietly. 'You know, I'm pretty sure Michael's single.'

'What?'

Frankie jumped as Sandy laughed.

'Oh, come on. He's no Hollywood heartthrob, but there's something incredibly charming about Michael. He's good and he's kind and he's—'

'Clever,' Frankie murmured.

Sandy gave her a more knowing look this time over the rim of her lemonade glass.

'Did you ever date a Hollywood heartthrob?' she asked with a wistful sigh, returning to her chips.

'Nope.'

Sandy looked up sharply.

'Never?'

'No. Actors are... Well, a lot of them are...' Frankie searched for the right word. 'Egotistical,' she decided. 'Especially when they've gotten to a certain stage in their career.'

'That makes sense.' Sandy sighed again. 'Still, there's quite a few I wouldn't kick out of bed. You weren't ever tempted just for the sex?'

Frankie laughed.

'Nope. I need more than a six pack to tempt me into bed. Or even a boat-load of talent, and I worked with some very lovely, talented people. No, I always found myself drawn to men behind the camera.'

'Directors? Producers? Writers?'

'Camera operators,' said Frankie, and Sandy pulled a face.

'Seriously?'

'Seriously. Not all of them, but they were all doing something similar, I guess. A man who knows what wire does what, who understands how the sound works on a film set, who knows what button does what.'

'Oh.' Sandy grinned to herself. 'That kind of man. You put it that way, they do sound better in bed.'

Frankie agreed.

'I mean, I have no Hollywood hunk to compare it to, but yeah, you see my point.'

'I do. I'm surprised none of them worked out.'

Frankie shrugged.

'None of them wanted to move to the UK with me. Certainly not to Scotland. They were all used to California sunshine by that point. They said we could go on holiday to Scotland, to see some snow, but that was it. And that was never going to be enough for me.'

This time, Sandy nodded enthusiastically.

'Absolutely. I couldn't leave Scotland. Well, not yet. Maybe when I'm older. I'd quite like to retire to Europe.'

'Oh?'

'Hmm. Spain.'

There was a pause as they ate their lunches and Frankie considered the merits of retiring to Spain. She was about to ask what their winters were like – she couldn't fathom a warm Christmas – when Sandy asked, 'So, are you going to ask Michael out?'

'What?' Frankie coughed, nearly choking on her mouthful. 'No. I don't know. Am I? No. Why?'

Sandy was grinning again, enjoying the redness of Frankie's cheeks.

'You should. You could ask him for a drink here. Then you're close to home, whether it goes well or not.' Then Sandy gave Frankie a wink and Frankie stared at her.

'Don't wink at me about that,' she said after a moment, and Sandy threw back her head and laughed, making a few of the men in the pub turn to look at them. Frankie sank back in her chair.

'He's been single as long as I've known him, I think,' Sandy continued, tucking back into her sandwich. 'So I would say you'll miss your moment, but I don't think that's a risk.'

'Sounds like he'd say no if I asked him out, then. Maybe he's not looking for that sort of thing.'

Sandy shrugged and finished off her sandwich.

'Perhaps. Still worth a shot.'

'And which vet would I go to if he turns me down?' Frankie asked, eating her last chip.

'You know Lily's not your dog.'

Frankie hesitated.

'Good point.'

'So what's the worst that could happen?'

Frankie opened and closed her mouth.

'See, the worst that could happen is you find someone else,' Sandy said.

'True.'

'What are you doing for Christmas?'

Frankie blinked at the sudden change in subject.

'Erm, not a lot. Why?'

'Drinks in the pub, that's why. But I want you to ask Michael out before then. And if you don't, I'll ask him for you.'

Frankie's eyes widened.

'You wouldn't.'

'Why not? Look, I think you'd make a great couple, and you do like him, don't you?' Sandy stared right into Frankie's eyes and Frankie couldn't help but nod.

'I do,' she admitted.

'Good. So that's that. Christmas drinks on Christmas Eve Eve right here, I'll let you know the time. Your parents are invited too, of course.'

Frankie nodded and murmured a thanks as her mind span and whirred with the terrifying notion of not only holding a conversation with Michael, if she could even catch a moment alone with him, but actually asking him out on a date.

Eighteen

December always moved so quickly. Suddenly they were halfway through the month and the last week of December was a write off, thanks to Christmas and New Year. Michael was rushing through job descriptions and meetings with his HR manager, who also happened to be his only HR employee. She was thrilled; it had been a while since she'd gotten her teeth into some new job descriptions. Michael considered asking her if she was over-worked at all, but his accountant had explained that they only had enough funds for two new posts, and if he was going to delegate properly, he needed to recruit two head vets. He glanced out of the main windows in the waiting room, over the road to the pub where Sandy was meeting with Frankie. Hiring two head vets would technically mean he would have more spare time. Time he could dedicate to a relationship, if he wanted to.

Michael gave a heavy sigh, his gaze searching the pub windows for any sign of Frankie, but there were only hazy figures on the other side of the glazing. Ripping his attention back to his currently empty practice, he checked the floors were clean and considered the potential of going for a walk to clear his head.

'There's a rumour going around that you're hiring a head vet.'

Michael looked up to find Ruby, the practice's only full-time vet, watching him from the reception desk. She took Sandy's seat and brushed some crumbs from the desk.

'It's true,' Michael admitted.

'At this practice?'

Ruby had a strong Scottish accent and a dark bob that framed her face. Her wife was a farmer in the Highlands and Michael was always waiting for Ruby to hand her notice in. How they spent so much time apart was beyond him.

'Yes.' Michael sighed and wandered closer, leaning on the other side of the reception desk. Ruby watched him expectantly. 'One here and one in the city,' he added. 'Would you be interested in a head vet position here?'

Ruby nodded.

'I would.'

Michael bit his lip.

'How do you do it?' he murmured.

Ruby frowned.

'Do what?'

'Spend so much time away from home.'

She softened and smiled.

'I spend every weekend at home.' She shrugged. 'It's not that bad. And some relationships do better with space. Have you ever lived on a farm?'

Michael shook his head.

'A lot of poo,' said Ruby. 'And death. That's basically farm living.'

'I always thought it might be interesting to become a livestock vet,' Michael said quietly.

Ruby shook her head.

'I'd rather be looking after a dog that someone loves so much they'd give them their own kidney if they could than an animal who was literally put on this planet to serve humans with its body. Do you know that cows, given a chance of a happy field, food and friends, dance and play? They're such big, bold personalities. And a lot of farmers care about them, sure, but I've met a fair few who know them only by numbers and how much they're worth.'

'I guess it's best not to become attached,' Michael mused.

Again, Ruby shrugged.

'If it doesn't sit well with you, why did you marry a farmer?' he asked. 'Does she sell her cows for meat?'

'Yes. She's a dairy farmer, and where do you think the boy calves go?' Ruby shuddered. 'I've been a vegan since I was five.'

Michael raised an incredulous eyebrow.

'But you married a dairy farmer.'

Ruby looked him in the eye.

'You don't choose who you fall in love with.'

'No, that's true.' Michael caught himself glancing out of the window, back to the pub.

'Cards on the table,' Ruby continued, 'I want to keep working here until my wife decides to give it up. Another ten years, maybe, then our plan is to move to France to open a bed and breakfast.'

Michael gave Ruby a curious look.

'You know the French are big meat eaters?'

'Yes. But that's what the EuroStar is for.'

Michael laughed and shrugged.

'Fair enough. I'll have a chat with HR.'

'Does it mean you'll be coming to Bekburn less?'

'I don't think I can bear not coming here as much as I do now,' Michael said after a short, thoughtful pause. 'It seems that hiring head vets to lessen my workload won't stop the amount of travelling I do.'

'The heart wants what the heart wants, huh?'

Michael agreed and then turned as the door to the practice opened and Sandy entered.

'Oh good, I'm not late.'

'Congratulations on your promotion,' said Ruby, standing and giving Sandy a wide grin. 'About time you were put in charge around here.'

Sandy laughed and gave a mock salute.

'Don't worry, I won't make any big changes.' She glanced at Michael, seemingly remembering that she was standing next to her boss. Pressing her lips together, Sandy made her way through reception, towards the back and the staff kitchenette. Ruby gave Michael a friendly smile and vanished into her consultation room. Glancing over his shoulder to the empty road, Michael wondered which way Frankie had gone and then followed Sandy into the kitchenette.

'How was your lunch?'

'Very nice,' said Sandy, making herself a cup of tea. She made a gesture to ask if he wanted one but he declined. Still, he stood in the doorway, fretting a little, wondering how to ask the questions that were on the tip of his tongue. When he looked up, Sandy was studying him.

'Frankie's lovely, isn't she?' she said slowly.

It felt like a trick question, so Michael only gave a short nod in response, and then, when that didn't seem enough, a low, 'Hmm.'

'Can you believe she's never dated a Hollywood star? I would have, if I was her and I'd had her career. Even if it was just one date, one night.'

Michael blinked, his mind immediately going to the idea of one date and one night with Frankie.

'Turns out she prefers the engineers and clever thinkers to the muscles,' Sandy added, stirring her tea and disposing of the tea bag. She gave Michael a smile and wandered past him, back to the reception desk. Michael didn't follow her, nor did he watch her go. He remained in place, staring down at the floor, mulling over her words.

Frankie would be going home. It wouldn't take

much to go and knock on her door, or call her, to ask how the dog was doing and then invite her for a drink.

Michael shook the idea away; he only had her parents' number and knocking on her door was creepy. Running after her from the pub would have been too much, as well.

Sighing, Michael made himself a coffee on auto-pilot and went into his office to give it more thought, closing his door and leaving the sounds of the early afternoon rush behind him.

Nineteen

It had been two long days since Frankie had lunch with Sandy, and Frankie had found herself avoiding the high street for fear of bumping into Michael and feeling forced to ask him out. Not that she didn't want to, but she was determined to do it in her own time. Instead, she'd driven to the next town over to buy Christmas decorations and a large potted tree. The tree went outside the farmhouse and her father helped her to put the lights around it, along with some outdoor baubles she'd found online. Lily helped for a while before growing bored and deciding that following the builders in and out of the house was much more fun. Geoff soon put a stop to that and Lily took to lying by the front door to watch them instead.

As they were finishing, rain drops began falling from the darkening sky.

'More rain,' muttered Geoff.

'Hurray for Scotland,' said Frankie with a grin. 'It's why it's so beautiful and green here.'

Geoff had to agree, but he wasn't happy about it.

'Come on, Lily. Time for a cuppa and staring out at the rain until it stops.'

Frankie thanked her father for his help and watched as Lily followed him over to the cottage. He'd already strung Christmas lights along the frontage of the little house and as he approached the front door, the lights turned on. Frankie found her mother in the window and they waved to each other.

Sighing, Frankie looked up at the sky and closed her eyes as the rain began to fall harder.

Now what was she going to do?

Continuing to work outside seemed like a stupid idea, considering. There wasn't a great deal she could do in the house while the builders were in, unless she started on the floors upstairs. She could rip up the carpet on the stairs, it was the last carpet left in the house and would involve going step by step to remove each tac, nail and gripper, along with any surprises waiting for her beneath.

Frankie pulled a face. She didn't fancy doing that with a load of builders in the house, and she couldn't ignore the desperate need deep down inside that she wanted to be out and about.

Fetching her car keys, she explained what she was doing to the builders, in case they needed to get hold of her, and then knocked on her parents' cottage door. Her mother answered, Lily zooming out and bouncing around Frankie as if she hadn't seen her for a week.

'I'm going into the city,' Frankie told her mother. 'I'll stay in touch.'

'In the rain?' Irene looked up at the sky. 'What about the roads?'

'I'll take it steady, don't worry.' Frankie kissed her mother's cheek. 'Bye, Dad!' she shouted through the cottage.

'Bye! Where're you going?' he shouted back.

'The city!' Frankie and Irene called back in unison.

'Be careful!'

Smiling to herself, Frankie quickly shed her warm coat and threw it onto the passenger seat of her car, climbed in and rolled slowly out of the driveway, tyres crunching on the gravel. She took a deep breath as she drove down the country roads, heading for the main road to Edinburgh. The trees on either side were mostly stripped of their leaves, spindly outlines against the dark grey sky. Puddles had already formed and the car's headlights shone across them before the tyres splashed through. Frankie went through them slowly if she couldn't avoid them, and searched the radio stations for something interesting.

Eventually she found a station playing Christmas songs, so she turned it up and let the music fill the car. With the darkness brewing outside, the swish-swish of the windscreen wipers and warmth blasting from the car's heater, it was almost a cosy journey to the main road. With all this rain, Frankie doubted there would be snow this Christmas. But there was already a faint coat of snow on the hills. That was enough. They certainly never had a white Christmas in London, so snowy hills would be perfect. The roads would still be clear, but the view would be Christmassy.

Smiling to herself, Frankie joined the main road, put her foot down and headed through the rain to Edinburgh.

Leaving her car in the Ingliston Park and Ride, Frankie bought a return ticket for the tram and waited for the next one to show up. It didn't take long. Frankie sat close to people with suitcases and heavy bags, having just landed at the airport, and stared out of the window as they travelled into the city. The rain was beating down now, and while Frankie had her thick winter coat, hat and an umbrella, she didn't fancy her chances of wandering around the city. As the tram stopped at Murrayfield, Frankie cast her gaze over the stadium and then, when no one got on or off, she took out her phone. It had been a few days since she'd checked her emails. Going from checking her emails every ten minutes to leaving her career and finding some peace had been mind-blowing, to the point where she now often forgot she had emails.

Her heart jolted as, among the junk, the name of her agent stood out in her inbox.

'Damn,' she muttered under her breath. She opened the email and read it quickly. Frowning, she read it again, slower this time.

Tapping her phone against her thigh, Frankie waited until the tram reached Haymarket, where she stepped off, marched towards West End, following the tram tracks, and called her agent.

Isy was one of the nicest people in the entertainment industry that Frankie had ever met. If it hadn't been for Isy signing her, Frankie reckoned her acting career would have been short and painful. While it was true that Isy always seemed to find her work, it was more that she was protective. She was a bouncy, talking a mile a minute, protective lioness. That was how Frankie had always seen her. Ultimately, the most efficient, professional and sometimes quite scary in the friendliest of ways person. Which was why, despite Frankie having quit, Isy had emailed her a list of job opportunities and Frankie was now calling to decline each and every one of them.

'Even the podcasts? I mean, I understand the TV work. I thought I'd include those just in case, but what's wrong with the podcast interview requests?'

Frankie sighed.

'Why are they inviting me on? I don't have anything to promote. What would I talk about?'

'Well, they just want to know what you're up to

right now. And what things were like.'

'Exactly. They want me to spill the beans, but there aren't any beans to spill. They'll be disappointed. I'm not the movie star they're looking for.'

'Of course you are! You can just have a fun chat, talk about the work you've done, what it meant to you, what it meant for other people. Your experiences of the panels at Comic-Con.'

Frankie's eye twitched at the mention.

'You know,' Isy continued, 'if you want something to promote, you could write a book about your experiences as an actor.'

'Nope!'

This wasn't the first time Isy had tried to convince Frankie to write a book.

'Well, what are you up to now? You must be working on something. Years living in London doing up that house, and all those possible TV and podcast opportunities on your doorstep and nothing.'

'I'm renovating my new house,' said Frankie.

'Is that the big house?'

'An old farmhouse, yes, it's quite big.'

'And you still don't want to get a production company involved? Renovation shows are all the rage right now.'

Frankie gave a small growl and then smiled as the man walking past gave her a look.

'Absolutely not. No production companies, no TV shows, no podcasts and no books. Okay?'

There was a pause down the line, long enough for Frankie to wonder if she'd lost connection.

'Frankie, what are you going to do once the house is finished?'

'I-I don't know.' Frankie slowed her frantic walking and found herself on Princes Street, looking up at the castle. Crossing the road, she carefully made her way down the slippery steps into the gardens. 'I don't know,' she breathed.

'So, I'll keep those podcast requests on hold?'

Frankie stopped and closed her eyes.

'Just in case you change your mind?' Isy continued when Frankie didn't respond. 'You know, when the house is done?'

'What if I just become a property developer?' Frankie mused, her eyes still closed. The darkness behind her eyelids offered no solace, although it was nice to shut the world out for a moment. She opened her eyes and walked slowly through the park towards the art galleries in the middle.

'With no production company or book?' Isy checked.

'Exactly.'

This time, Isy paused.

'You don't want more money coming in? Just in case?'

Frankie laughed, making a young couple near her jump.

'No. I think I'm good.'

'What if you run out?'

'How? On all the lavish parties and expensive cars and toy boys?'

'Are toy boys still a thing?'

'Probably not. But maybe they are if you're into lavish parties and expensive cars. My point is, I think I'm okay. And if I do change my mind and decide to do anything worth selling to the general public, I'll let you know.'

'I'll be the first to know?'

Frankie smiled.

'Of course.'

'Fine. I submit. You win this round.'

'This round?'

'Are there any toy boys?'

'Is, I'm in my late thirties. A toy boy would have to be early twenties, wouldn't he? Yuck.'

Isy laughed.

'Fair enough. What about a man? Have you met a gorgeous Scottish hunk in a kilt yet?'

The idea of Michael in a kilt flashed before Frankie and she shook it away.

'No.'

'No?'

'No.'

'Are you sure? Because there was a hesitation and a faint question mark there.'

Frankie sighed, looking back up to the castle.

'There might be someone, but nothing official.' She didn't even know if Michael would say yes to her, she really had no idea if he was interested.

'Exciting!' Isy shrilled. 'Well, London is the same old, so if anything does happen there with Mr Scottish, please let me know. I could use a bit of sexy good news.'

'Sexy good news?' Frankie smirked, walking up the steps out of the gardens and onto the road. She turned right and started walking up the Mound.

'Okay, fine. Romantic good news. Is that better? Are you all right? You sound like you're having sexy good times right now.'

'Isy! I'm walking up one of Edinburgh's really steep roads. In the rain.' Frankie tried not to puff, but her lungs screamed objections.

'You'll be fit when I next see you, at least.'

'Definitely that.'

'And maybe with a sexy Scottish man on your arm?'

'Maybe.' Frankie grinned.

'Take care, Frankie,' said Isy, her tone almost wistful. 'Let me know if you change your mind.'

They said their goodbyes and when she hung up, Frankie's chest tightened. Was Isy right? Maybe she should be grabbing these opportunities, going on podcasts, meeting new people, writing a book. It would have given her something solid to do while she waited for the builders to finish.

Pursing her lips, Frankie made her way down the Royal Mile and stopped in a coffee shop to catch her breath and eat a quick lunch. Then she ventured down the George IV Bridge towards the Edinburgh

Central Library where there was reprieve from the rain, some warmth and books, so Frankie could give these thoughts serious consideration and maybe learn more about writing.

The library closed at five o'clock, which is when Frankie left. Glancing up at the beautiful wrought iron gates that marked the entrance, she paused on the road. The afternoon had flown by and her head was spinning. It was still raining, although it was less hurried than earlier and more settled in. She joined the crowds, getting carried along until they dropped her back on the Royal Mile. There, she popped in a tourist shop and bought herself a Scottish-themed notebook and a very red tartan pen, before hurrying down the road to the nearest Starbucks. She bought a bucket of coffee and a muffin, and curled up in a corner to scribble notes. Her mother messaged her to let her know the builders had gone for the day, and Frankie responded with a photo of her coffee and muffin.

An hour and a half later, all of Frankie's thoughts were in the notebook and her coffee and muffin were gone. She had more research to do, people to email, questions that needed answering, but things were starting to get clearer. She glanced down at the figures and scribbles across the pages, a plan emerging of purpose and a good use for the zeroes in her bank accounts. She closed the notebook with a small sigh.

The sun had long set behind the thick clouds, leaving the city in a shrouded darkness. It had also stopped raining, which was a blessing. Her stomach rumbling, Frankie considered her options. She should go home, but she was hungry for something more substantial than another muffin. She could eat first, but then she'd get home so late.

She walked as she thought, up the road towards the castle, glancing at the expensive restaurants as she passed them. She wasn't in the mood for posh food. There was a McDonald's near Princes Street and a tram stop, that would do her. Except that she found her feet taking her up to the castle instead. She went with them, aware that the castle would be beautifully lit up with its Christmas display. Most of the crowds near the castle were gone by the time Frankie reached it and she took some photos on her phone of the castle with the cloudy night sky behind it. As she walked back down, her eye was caught by the tempting lights of the Witchery.

Frankie had always wanted to venture inside, but had been put off by the menu and the fear of being out of place in such an expensive looking restaurant. The building was so old, the history and memories in the stone seeped out whenever Frankie walked past, or that's how it felt. She stopped at the menu on the wall outside and asked her stomach if it fancied anything listed.

Twenty

It was too late to back out now. Michael checked his reflection one last time before grabbing his keys and glancing back to the living room, where Agnes was sitting on the piano in her favourite spot, watching him.

'What am I supposed to do?' he asked her. 'Just not go?'

Agnes did a slow blink at him.

'Feign illness?' he muttered, and then stopped. He could feign an illness. Michael shook his head. Dane would see right through that. In fact, hadn't Michael feigned illness on the last date Dane and Milly had set him up on?

Sighing, Michael glanced at his reflection again. His hair was still in place, his shirt collar was neatly folded, he didn't have a big stain down his front or a cold coming on or a big spot growing on his nose.

'It might go better than I think,' he told Agnes. 'Maybe this woman will make me forget about Frankie.'

Agnes gave him a look of disdain, or maybe that was just her face. It was hard to tell with this light and topic of conversation.

'Wish me luck, then, I guess. I probably won't be out too late.' He gave Agnes a wave and locked the door behind him. As he made it onto the street, Michael glanced up at the windows to his apartment. He'd left a light on in the living room, giving a cosy glow through the window and a vague outline of a fluffy cat. Michael resisted the urge to wave, turned back to look where he was going and practised saying hello in his head.

Hello, it's lovely to meet you. You look lovely.

No, he'd said lovely too many times.

His father had once told him that there was never any denying that animals were easier than humans. Michael had scoffed. Humans are animals, he'd told his father. There's no difference. His father had only laughed and then, once, warned Michael that one day he'd see.

'I see, Dad,' he murmured as he walked towards Princes Street Gardens. It was dark and the main road was heaving with people leaving work, making their way home, or stepping off the bus or tram ready for an early evening of Christmas shopping, going out to dinner, or whatever the kids did these days. It was also full of tourists.

Sometimes Michael enjoyed watching people discover and enjoy his city, taking photos where millions had stood before them to take the exact same photo. He assumed social media was full of the same thing over and over, but he hoped those photos were more for family and friends, being told of the magic of Edinburgh.

Other times, Michael had to stop himself from sighing and swearing as tourists bustled into him without an apology. Didn't they understand that this was also home to a lot of people?

'Hey there, Rory.' Michael stopped at a bench where a man was sitting, his Labrador lying at his feet. The dog's tail wagged hard at the sight of Michael, so he crouched and gave the dog a cuddle.

'Hi, Michael. Fancy seeing you out here. You look sharp.'

'Thanks. I'm being set up on a blind date by some friends.'

Rory looked up at him with watery blue eyes and laughed.

'You sound like you'd rather you had other friends.'

'They keep doing this.' Michael grinned and gave a shrug. 'Keep telling me this time it'll be different.'

'Maybe it will.'

'Can I?'

Rory nodded and Michael sat beside him on the bench.

'How's it going?' he asked. He'd met Rory and his dog, Bob, three months ago when a woman had passed on Michael's business card and explained that he offered free treatment for pets living rough.

Bob had been in good health, but Michael had made sure he was wormed and vaccinated, and given him a toy and a new warm coat for the cold nights. He was wearing the coat now and it still looked in good shape.

'As good as it can, I guess.'

'Nowhere's come through yet, huh?' Michael asked, rubbing Bob's ears.

'No, but I know where to get a hot meal at Christmas. So that's something.'

Michael sighed hard.

'I wish I could help more,' he muttered. 'I don't know what to do. If I owned a hotel, you'd have a room.'

Rory smiled at Michael.

'You already do enough. I can't tell you how much I appreciate it. Knowing that Bobby's okay. That's half the battle.'

Michael bit down on his tongue to stop the hot tears burning at the back of his eyes. Then he dug into his pocket and pulled out some notes.

'To be honest, I was hoping I'd bump into you.' That was partially a lie. He'd been hoping he would bump into someone. 'Here. I know it's not much.' He handed Rory a hundred pounds in twenties. 'Get some food and drink, or maybe a night somewhere warm and dry. Whatever you want. And come round to the practice tomorrow and I'll give you some more food for Bobby, if you need it yet?'

Rory stared at the money and then looked up at

Michael.

'Are you sure?'

'Of course I am. Please. Take it for me. You can do whatever you like with it.'

Rory nodded and took the money.

'Thanks.'

'Just, be safe with it. Keep it hidden. All that stuff.'

Rory nodded again and stashed the money deep into his pocket.

'Good. Take care, and you're always welcome at my practice. Okay?' Michael said it to Rory but he was giving Bob a farewell ear rub.

'Thanks, Michael. Really. For all of it.'

Michael could only nod.

'Oh, hey, good luck with the date!'

Stopping in his tracks, Michael laughed.

'Thanks! I'll need it.'

He continued walking through the park, up to the galleries, where he turned right onto the Mound. He side-stepped tourists, pausing to take photos, chatting to one another, not looking where they were going, and brushed past residents, rushing to get to wherever they were headed. All the while, he thought about Rory and Bob instead of his upcoming date.

If only he owned a hotel. That's what had fallen out of his mouth. It wasn't a hotel he would need, though, was it. It was a hostel. Michael pulled a face. Perhaps a cross between the two. Somewhere with rooms and safety, where pets were welcome, and a restaurant on site, along with a vet practice, of course. Michael shook his head, smiling to himself. The red tape for such a thing would probably be as enormous as the amount of money he'd need. He would never be able to afford such a thing, but then who could? Wasn't that what investors were for?

By the time Michael broke from his thoughts, he found that he'd walked up the steep path from the Mound to the Royal Mile. He stopped to catch his breath and then spotted Dane and Milly with a woman standing on the other side of the road. Michael stepped back, hiding behind the suddenly welcome shield of tourists leaving the castle esplanade. The woman looked nice enough. She had long blonde hair and large eyes, and her red lips were partially hidden by a huge scarf. She was wearing a long coat, but it hugged her figure, and there were heels on her feet. Michael had no idea how anyone walked in heels on these cobbles. She was laughing nervously at something Dane had said, and glancing around. Was she looking for Michael? Would she know him if she saw him?

Michael sighed and studied her face as best he could given the distance and people walking between them. She was pretty. Pretty and nervous. He was nervous, too. Surely that had to be a good start?

Michael's heart jolted as his eyes travelled along

the front of the restaurant. He froze, holding his breath.

He'd dreamed of her before he met her, she'd appeared randomly before him in the city, to the point where he couldn't get her out of his head. It was all a coincidence. Michael certainly didn't believe in any kind of spell his mother and her friends may have done.

But here, at the moment and place where Michael was to meet a date, was Frankie Taylor, studying the menu of the same restaurant he would soon be entering.

It couldn't be a coincidence. When did a coincidence stop being a coincidence and become something more?

Michael couldn't take his eyes from her.

This is the moment, a small voice in the back of his mind told him. This is it.

Michael cut across the crowd of tourists moving in front of him and approached Frankie from the opposite side to where his friends and date were waiting.

'Frankie?'

Frankie jumped and turned, horror in her eyes. She visibly relaxed when she saw Michael.

'Oh, thank god. I mean, hi!' A new panic hit her eyes, but it was too late, she was already smiling a smile that made Michael's heart pound.

'Sorry, I didn't mean to creep up on you.'

'Oh, it's okay. I was miles away. Just looking at

the menu.'

'Are you...eating here tonight?'

'No. No, I don't think so. I've just always wanted to go inside, but this is all a little too posh for me. I'm more of a steakhouse girl, you know?' Frankie gave a small laugh, looking Michael up and down. 'Are you eating here tonight?'

Michael gave a slow nod, wishing upon wish that Frankie was the date he was there to meet.

'I'm having dinner with friends. They've...they've set me up on a blind date.' He gave something of a laugh. 'I was wishing I'd backed out, but I'm glad I bumped into you.'

'Oh?'

Michael was certain that Frankie's eyes had dulled at the mention of a blind date.

'Yes. Would you... Erm... That is, would you, maybe, someday...' Michael cleared his throat. For crying out loud, pull yourself together and just ask her!

'Would you like to go for a drink sometime? Or get lunch with me? In the city, or in Bekburn. Whatever you prefer.' Michael stopped any more words spilling out, acutely aware of Frankie's eyes widening along with her smile as he spoke.

'I'd love to,' she told him, and his stomach flipped. Grinning before he could stop himself, he dug his fingernails into his palms to keep from reacting further.

'Wonderful!'

'Can I just check,' said Frankie carefully.

'Of course.'

'Are you asking me because your mother told you to?'

Michael hesitated. He'd be lying if he said no.

'Is this a "welcome to Edinburgh" offer, or are you asking me out on a date?' Frankie clarified, smiling as she watched Michael's expression.

'Oh, the latter.'

Frankie grinned, and the rest of the world vanished.

'Good. Good. Okay, then yes. That would be great. When are you next in Bekburn?' Frankie fumbled in her pocket and brought out her phone. 'Wait, do you already have my number? From the vets?'

'No, I have your parents' number, and it would be unprofessional to use that.'

Michael lifted his gaze to meet Frankie's eyes. There was a pause as she smiled at him, then she handed him her phone.

'Here. Put your number in.'

He did as he was told, all the while wondering if he should admit that the number he gave her on a Post-it the day Lily was rushed to him was the same number he was putting into her phone. He'd meant to write down the number for the city practice, but his hand had decided otherwise.

'How about tomorrow, if you're free? We could do lunch. Here, if you like?' he offered, handing her phone back.

'That'd be amazing. Should I meet you here? Do we need to book? What time can you do?' She hesitated and glanced up at him. 'Sorry.' She smiled and pressed her screen. Michael's phone vibrated in his pocket. She waved her phone at him, showing that she was calling him, then she hung up.

'There's my number.'

Michael, breathless, smiled and managed, 'I'll see if I can book us a table. I'll let you know, but sometime between twelve and one?'

'Sure, let me know and I'll see you then.' Frankie nodded, and there was another pause as they both watched one another. 'I'll, erm, let you get on with your friends, then. And your...date.' Frankie bit her lower lip, not taking her eyes from Michael as he shuddered back into the real world.

'Right. The date.' He glanced away from her, towards his friends. Dane had spotted him but hadn't told the women in the group. Instead, he gave Michael a curious look.

'Please don't worry about that,' he added quietly, looking back to Frankie.

She gave a soft smile and nodded.

'Okay. And maybe tomorrow, over lunch, you can tell me what on earth tomato jam is?' She turned and pointed to the tomato jam on the menu.

Michael laughed a little too loud and snapped his mouth shut.

'It's like strawberry jam, but with tomatoes and

less sugar.'

'Sounds revolting.'

'I won't get you a pot of it, then.'

They studied each other's eyes, both smiling helplessly.

Frankie broke from the spell first, glancing over Michael's shoulder and whispering, 'See you tomorrow. Have fun, but not too much.'

She left. Slipping into the lessening crowds of tourists. Michael went to watch her go, but then came Dane's voice.

'Mike? You all right there?'

He turned to find the group approaching him.

'There you are!' he said. 'Yes, sorry, hello!' He reached out an arm to hug Milly and politely shake the hand of the blonde woman – Rachel – and tell her she looked lovely, before following them into the restaurant. Dane put some distance between them and the women and then whispered over his shoulder, 'Who was she?'

'Tell you later,' Michael whispered back.

Dane glanced at him.

'This date is a waste of time, then?'

'Sorry.'

Dane laughed and clapped his hands.

'No worries,' he murmured. 'Tonight's on me!' he declared as they took their seats.

Twenty-One

The next morning was the longest of Frankie's life, and that included all the early starts to sit in a chair for makeup before the sun had risen. Frankie rushed towards the Royal Mile from the nearest tram stop. She'd hardly slept, had woken early to leave out cupcakes for the builders before accompanying her father on a dog walk and wiling away the morning hours. After all that, now she might be late. She'd planned on taking the long route, to give herself time to catch her breath, but that plan had gone out the window long ago.

The sky had lightened throughout the morning and turned from a dark grey to almost blue as white clouds passed slowly overhead. The wind was still cold and Frankie had a scarf wrapped around her neck and face, warming her nose every time she breathed out in a rush of nerves.

Avoiding the crowds going to and from the castle, Frankie spotted a lone figure of a man bundled in a coat, reading the Witchery's menu, just as she had been doing the day before. His back was to Frankie, but still she recognised Michael. He turned, glancing down the road, and his eyes lit up when he saw her. Stomach flipping, Frankie grinned and strode towards him.

'Hi,' she managed, her mouth dry.

'H-hi.' He stuttered a little on that small word, his eyes darting over her once and then down to the ground. She watched, softening at the sight, resisting the urge to reach out to him.

'Sorry I'm late.' She sucked in air, trying to appear fitter than she was.

'Oh, no. You're bang on time.' Michael gave a small, nervous laugh and then almost frowned at himself.

Frankie smiled and looked up at the restaurant, hardly believing she was finally going to go inside.

'Shall we go get warm?' Michael offered, leading her to the entrance. She followed him in and a wonderful, dark warmth hit her. The restaurant wasn't full, but neither was it empty. There was a gentle murmur of conversation and Frankie became aware that she'd need to keep her voice down. The dining room itself was beautiful, with small historic features everywhere she looked.

They were taken to their table and handed menus, which Frankie scanned a few times, trying to subdue the panic of being somewhere so posh.

'What did you try last night?' she asked without thinking, before snapping her mouth shut.

'I had the fillet of beef,' said Michael. 'But this is a lunch menu.'

Frankie pressed her lips together, desperately reading the menu again, hoping the words would change. Her mouth dry, she glanced up to find Michael studying her. 'Do you not like anything on there?' he whispered.

'Erm...'

'You did say you're more of a steakhouse girl,' Michael added quietly, with such a sweet smile that Frankie almost leaned across the table to kiss him.

Instead, she gave a meek nod, looking back to the menu.

'Would you like to go somewhere else?' came his whisper.

Frankie inhaled deep and held it.

'You're allowed to say yes.'

She laughed, exhaling in a rush.

'I guess I just wasn't expecting the menu to be quite so... I mean, a poached hen's egg? That means a poached egg. It's not going to be a cockerel's egg, is it?'

'I think it's instead of a quail's egg.'

'Oh. Yeah, see, I don't come from places where I immediately think of quail,' said Frankie gently, her cheeks burning.

'Or duck,' said Michael, his lips twitching in a smile.

Frankie watched him, relieved that he was only teasing.

'I've just never seen a chicken egg described as a hen's egg,' she told him, leaning across the table.

He leaned forward so they could whisper conspiratorially in the quiet restaurant.

'There are other places we could go,' he told her.

'No, no. That would be rude.' Frankie sat back, hating herself a little. 'I can eat here.' She gazed over the menu again. Her choices were deer, seafood or roasted pumpkin.

She pulled a face just as the waitress came over to take their order. Michael gave Frankie an almost panicked look, so she gathered herself and put everything she'd learned in Hollywood into practice.

'Do you have a dessert menu?' she asked.

'We do, but—'

'Can I see that, please?'

'You wouldn't like a starter? Or a main?'

'Darling, it's Thursday. I don't do starters or mains on a Thursday.' Frankie swallowed a laugh that threatened to come up, aware that she may have taken it too far.

The waitress gave her a look, left and returned with a dessert menu.

'You're just having a pudding?' Michael asked.

Frankie nodded.

'Oh yes, a bitter chocolate torte with caramelised pear ice cream is better than pumpkin, deer and seafood any day,' she told him before looking up the wait-ress. 'The chocolate torte, please. You can have whatever you like, though,' she added to Michael. 'Please have a main or something.'

She sat back, her fingers trembling as the waitress turned her attention to Michael. He studied Frankie, although she only briefly met his eyes.

'Two spoons?' he suggested.

A grin bloomed on Frankie's face, her body relaxing at once.

'And two spoons,' she agreed. 'And I'll have the fresh lemonade.'

'Oh, that sounds good. Me too,' said Michael.

The waitress took their menus and left, shaking her head, to prepare them a lemonade each.

'She's going to tell everyone about us,' Frankie whispered. 'I'm so sorry.'

'Don't be ridiculous. This is already the most fun I've ever had on a date.'

Frankie met Michael's gaze and he immediately sank back.

'I mean... This is a date, though, isn't it?'

'Of course it is,' said Frankie gently. 'Speaking of which, how did last night go?'

Michael's eyes widened and Frankie couldn't help but laugh.

'That well, huh?'

'I'm sorry,' said Michael. 'About all of that. My friends are always trying to set me up on dates and sometimes it's just easier to agree and go along—'

'Hey, it's okay,' said Frankie. 'I get it. You're allowed to say yes to dates when you're single. How did it go?'

'Oh, erm... It was all right,' said Michael, staring back down at the table. 'I thought of you when my friend ordered the tomato jam.'

Frankie laughed.

'Have you actually tried it?'

'I have.'

'Would you try it again?'

'Probably not.'

Frankie's heart pounded as his soft eyes met hers.

'Do you think you'll see her again?' Frankie asked quietly.

Michael's gaze didn't falter.

'No.'

Frankie's breath caught in her throat, and she pulled her eyes away as the waitress returned with their drinks.

'How are you finding Bekburn? Are you settling in well?'

Frankie nodded as she swallowed a mouthful of lemonade and put the glass down, fighting to stop her face contorting at the sweet sourness of it.

'Hmm. Yes. It's gorgeous. My parents moved up with me – as you know – they're loving it too. Just this morning my dad was saying how the fresh Scottish air is getting him up earlier.'

Michael nodded, sipping his own drink.

'And you've been coming into the city a lot?'

'Oh, yes. Edinburgh is my favourite place in the

world. I very nearly bought a place in the city, but then I saw the farmhouse and its cottage, and all that potential, and I couldn't say no to it.'

Michael's smile seemed to fade a little and Frankie's internal alarm bells sounded.

'Are you okay?'

'Hmm? Oh, yes, why?'

'You didn't seem happy when I mentioned buying a place in the city. Or the farmhouse. Was it the farmhouse?'

Something in Michael's features twitched and then he sighed, relenting and sitting back a little.

'I'm sorry. I didn't mean that to show. I thought about buying the farmhouse when it came on the market, but decided against it.'

Frankie watched him carefully.

'And now you regret it?'

'A little. Maybe. I don't know. I still haven't decided if I want to move out of the city. And the farmhouse is so big, and such a big project. How are you getting on with it?'

'Fine. Good. We're going to extend my parents' cottage and I'm currently rebuilding a big kitchen diner. It's a lot of work, but it's going to be amazing.' Her mind was racing, replaying Michael's words and the twitch at his lips over and over.

'I would never have managed any of that. I'm glad it's in your hands and not mine.' He gave her a sweet smile and Frankie's thoughts calmed.

'Is that why you asked me to lunch?' she asked

quietly, the words slipping out before she could stop them.

Michael's eyes widened.

'Oh. No, no. It's not like that.'

'Okay.'

'I asked you to lunch because...'

Frankie watched him struggle, his gaze dropping back to the table.

'I'm glad you asked me,' she told him, leaning forward.

His eyes lifted.

'You are?'

Frankie nodded.

'I thought maybe I should ask you, but I've never been good at that sort of thing.'

A smile touched the corners of Michael's mouth.

'No. Me neither.'

'But you managed it. You're braver than me.'

Michael narrowed his eyes a little, thoughtfully, studying her, and Frankie sat back under the heat of his gaze.

'Sandy tells me you were an actor in Hollywood. That sounds pretty brave to me.'

The loud laugh left Frankie without warning and she put a hand over her mouth to stop it.

'I guess. But I was younger then. People tend to be recklessly brave when they're young, don't they.'

Michael frowned and there was a pause as a chocolate torte with ice cream was placed between them, along with two spoons. Michael waited for

Frankie, so she chose a spoon and carefully slid it into the torte.

'I don't think I was ever recklessly brave,' he murmured.

'You run two veterinary practices. Oh my— This is gorgeous!' Frankie looked up, wondering if the waitress had heard her. She settled back, swallowing the mouthful and reaching forward for more. 'Sandy told me. About the two practices, about how you've been taking on so much, growing the business. And about the charity work you do.'

Michael gave a fond smile.

'Isn't it funny how Sandy has been talking about us to one another.'

'Funny,' Frankie agreed with a grin. 'Almost like she wanted us to go to lunch together.'

Michael lifted his eyes and held her gaze. The urge to squirm as heat rose through her body was almost too much, but Frankie stayed still, hoping she wasn't giving too much away.

'My father left me the city practice,' said Michael, returning to his food. 'And I was qualified long before then, so that wasn't brave, as such. Perhaps buying the practice in Bekburn was, but it didn't feel brave. It was more of a...relief.'

'How so?'

'To be out of the city. To be making my own decisions, perhaps.'

Frankie smiled.

'I know that feeling. I felt so lost when my

contracts ended and I stopped acting. I'd decided to quit years before but hadn't really given any thought to what would come next. For some reason, I thought the next thing would just present itself. And I suppose it sort of did. In a way.'

'What was that?'

'I bought an old Victorian house in London and renovated it. Did a lot of the work myself. It's why I wanted the farmhouse. It's a bigger project.'

'You want to do property renovation?'

'Maybe. I still haven't worked that one out. The property market is so...weird right now. You know? Everything's so expensive. It seems a bit disgusting to turn my hand to something just to take money and feed my own pockets, especially when I have enough savings to get by. Every time I read the news or go into the city, I'm reminded of how many people are struggling and don't have enough. I want to help, but I'm not sure how. Other than donating money, of course. I already do that. My agent wants me to write books and make TV shows and be on podcasts and stuff. I was thinking I could do all that and donate everything I earn to charity, but it still doesn't seem enough.' Frankie looked up at Michael. 'How did you get into your charity work?'

Michael smiled.

'I was asked,' he said simply. 'Truthfully, I was already doing what I do now, in a way. I was already offering people on the streets with pets to come to my practice if they had any concerns, and I would always treat their pets for free. Always. It made sense to accept an offer to join the charity when it was set up. Still, it's not enough.'

They both stared down at the almost eaten torte in thoughtful silence. Frankie glanced up at Michael without him noticing, wondering what good her money could do in his hands.

'Did you become a vet because of your dad?' she asked.

Michael nodded.

'I've always loved animals, of course. We were brought up around them. I loved that my father could often make them better or end their misery. I wanted to carry on his work, and work beside him, which I did for a long time. But sometimes I wonder if that was a mistake. I sort of feel a bit tied to the job now.'

'Like you'd be disappointing him if you stopped?'

Michael nodded and looked up to Frankie.

'What made you stop acting?'

Frankie gave a short laugh.

'Oh, you know, the usual. I hate flying and all my jobs were in North America for some reason. And the industry can be cruel. I've been told to lose weight more times than I can count.' Michael frowned, his gaze bouncing down to where Frankie's body vanished beneath the table. 'I was lucky it was nothing worse. And I didn't want to stick around to find out what horrors awaited. Plus, I got bored. It was time for something new. There's not a lot of creative freedom when you're part of a huge franchise being made by rich producers who only see money and nothing else.'

Michael's features lightened and he stared at Frankie with eyebrows raised.

'Oh dear. Have you told Sandy that? I can almost hear her cackling with glee over what gossip that talk could lead to.'

Frankie laughed.

'She's tried but so far not succeeded in getting actual gossip from me. I'm close to cracking, though. Please don't tell her that.'

Michael laughed and the sound made Frankie's stomach flip, her heart pounding. His smile was delicious but his laugh was something else. She wondered if she could get him to laugh again.

The torte went quickly, as did their drinks, so Frankie offered to pay and a small, polite argument followed, which Michael won. Determined, Frankie declared that she would pay next time. Michael smiled and agreed, leading Frankie back out onto the Royal Mile. She took a deep breath of the cold city air and felt sick to her stomach.

'Do you want some proper food?' came Michael's voice beside her.

'A sandwich or something would be good,' she agreed.

'I know a good place, but it's on the other side of the gardens.'

'Oh, I never say no to walking through Princes

Street Gardens,' said Frankie, flashing him a smile.

Given that this was his birth city, Frankie did her best to let Michael lead the way, down the steep hill, past the galleries, and down the steps into the gardens, heading towards St Cuthbert's church beneath the castle.

They walked slowly, which helped with Frankie's nausea, and chatted about pets they'd had and the mishaps Michael had seen during his long career as a vet. By the time they left the gardens, Frankie no longer felt sick. Just hungry.

'It's amazing what a dog will eat,' he finished as they reached a sandwich shop on the corner of a street.

'Lily was like that as a puppy. Always had to have something in her mouth,' Frankie said as Michael held the door open for her.

They bought a sandwich each and found a little table in the corner to sit and eat.

'Do you think it's strange, about our mothers meeting?' Frankie asked.

'Not if you know my mother,' said Michael quietly.

Once they'd eaten, Frankie sat back and sighed.

'Better?' Michael asked.

'Much. I'm sorry about all that. But, you know, this has been a lot of fun.'

'It has,' said Michael carefully, his eyes softening again.

'Do you live near your mother?' Frankie asked,

wondering what direction he would go in if they parted ways now.

'No. I live near here, actually. It's why I know about this place.'

'Oh? In the West End? How lovely. In one of the grand Victorian buildings? Are they Victorian or Georgian? Edwardian?'

Michael smiled.

'I own a flat in one of those types of buildings, yes.'

'Magical,' Frankie breathed. 'That's what I was considering buying.'

'A flat?'

'Well, no, a house.' Frankie closed her mouth, aware that her full stomach could get her into trouble.

'Do you... Would you like to...' Michael stopped and sighed.

'Are you trying to invite me back to yours?' Frankie asked, smiling and leaning forward as much as her stomach would allow.

Michael glanced up at her.

'That's too forward, isn't it.'

'I don't think so,' she said gently, wondering where on earth she was going with this. She wasn't going to sleep with this man on the first date. Was she? With a full stomach?

'In the spirit of property development and historic buildings, would you like to see my flat?' Michael asked, his voice low.

Frankie nodded, heat rushing through her.

They left the sandwich shop and walked almost in silence to Michael's flat. Climbing the stairs was a bit much, and Frankie was reminded of what she'd eaten and that not enough time had passed.

His flat was cosy and smelled of him. It was clean, but there was a hint of testosterone. And cat.

Frankie laughed when a big, fluffy cat jumped onto a chair beside her.

'That's Agnes,' said Michael, wandering over to scratch the cat's ears. Agnes purred, leaning against him. 'She came in as a stray one day in a very sorry state. I fixed her up and called the rescue centre to come get her, but then I just couldn't let her go. I ended up taking her home instead, and she's been here ever since.'

'That's so sweet,' said Frankie. 'Hello, Agnes.' She rubbed Agnes's ears and the cat purred louder. 'Why did you call her Agnes?'

'My mother named her. Said she looked like an Agnes.'

Frankie studied the cat.

'It does suit her.'

The cat left them, jumping down from the chair and wandering over to the piano by the window, leaping up to sit and stare out at the world.

Frankie's eyes widened.

'Do you play piano?'

'Oh, yes. My mother wanted me to be a classical pianist, but I had other ideas. It was meant to be another career choice, in case I decided against being a vet. Would you like a drink?'

'You had other ideas?' Frankie scoffed, following Agnes to the piano. 'But you still play? Do you still play classical? Is that the right way to ask that?' She looked back to Michael.

He pursed his lips a little and his cheeks reddened.

'No, I play jazz and blues. Mostly jazz.'

Somehow, Frankie's eyes widened further.

'Oh, that's amazing! Will you play for me?'

Michael hesitated.

'It's okay,' Frankie added. 'You don't have to.'

'I can't get you a drink?' Michael fidgeted.

'I'm okay, thanks.' Frankie was still full, running her fingers over the top of the piano.

Then Michael was behind her, and beside her, sitting down at the stool and placing his long fingers over the keys. He didn't speak a word but played as Frankie watched. Agnes laid down, relaxing as music filled the room.

'That was beautiful,' said Frankie when he finished. 'You're so talented.'

'Oh, no, that's just years of practice,' said Michael, standing quickly and brushing his hands together.

'No, no. That's talent,' said Frankie, unable to take her eyes from him. He finally looked back at her and she only then realised how close they were.

'Thank you,' he whispered. 'I've had an amazing

time today.' He leaned forward.

'Me too,' Frankie murmured, going up on tiptoe.

Their lips met for a tantalising moment, sending a jolt through Frankie. It was nothing more than a brush, a hint of what could be, a sensation of warmth against the outside chill.

Just as she was about to lift herself further, or reach out to pull him down to her, there was a short, sharp noise and they bounced apart.

Breathing hard and blinking, Michael pulled his phone from his pocket.

'Sorry, I'm sorry. Excuse me.' He answered the phone, lifting it to his ear.

Frankie, heart pounding, held her breath and waited, wondering where his bedroom was. Or if they could somehow have each other on the piano. No, it was too close to the window.

'Hmm... What time?'

Frankie snapped back to Michael, her full stomach lurching.

'Of course. I'm on my way.' He hung up and stared down at the piano.

'You have to go?' Frankie asked, her voice breaking a little.

'I'm so sorry,' said Michael, looking up at her. 'An emergency has come up.'

'There's no other vet to cover for you?'

'No. Not yet. I'm in the process of hiring someone. I'm so sorry,' he repeated, leaving her by the piano and reaching for his coat. 'Will you be okay getting home?'

'Of course, no worries.' Frankie was finding it hard to smile.

He rushed her out of the flat and left her on the pavement outside, without even a kiss on the cheek before he rushed away. Frankie watched him go, wrapping herself in a hug, the nausea returning as a gust of wind hit her.

Twenty-Two

As he strode towards his city practice, Michael swore to himself. He hadn't even given Frankie a kiss goodbye. One kiss wouldn't have taken much time. A word about doing it again, about how much fun he'd had wouldn't have hurt. What was wrong with him?

He'd message her later. Or when he got to the practice. Apologise, tell her he'd make it up to her. Frankie didn't leave his mind the entire way to the practice, but then, as soon as he was inside all thoughts of messaging her left his head. The vet on duty filled him in and they scrubbed up together as the nurses quickly prepared the cat for surgery. Her worried owners sat in the waiting room, where one of the receptionists was making them cups of tea. There wasn't a chance to message Frankie, even if Michael had remembered, and once he was in the surgery theatre, all his other thoughts quietened.

Three hours later, the cat was waking up and they had done all they could. Michael collapsed into his office chair and rubbed his hands over his face before checking the time.

'Cup of tea?' The head nurse wandered in with a cup which she placed on Michael's desk.

'Oh, thank you.' He reached for it immediately. 'How's the patient?'

'He's doing well, almost fully awake.'

'I'll come in and check on him in a bit.'

The head nurse left and Michael sat back, his fingers wrapped around the warm ceramic of the tea mug. Finally, his mind relaxed enough to show him a memory of Frankie's smile from that afternoon, his lips tingled as they had done during their almost kiss. How had that been today?

Michael pulled out his phone and stared at the blank screen. She hadn't messaged him, but why would she?

He jumped, nearly throwing his phone into his tea as it started ringing. Composing himself, pressing his lips together, he answered.

'Hi, Mum.'

'Are you free?'

Michael smiled.

'Just about. Are you all right?'

'Oh yes. Just back from the shops. When are you

back in the city?'

'Actually, now.'

'Oh, weren't you in Bekburn today?'

'Not today.' Michael struggled for a moment, and then he sighed. 'Mum, you know that spell you and your book club friends did for me?'

'...Yes.'

'Well... I bumped into Frankie yesterday and asked her out.'

His mother gasped, but he continued before she could ask anything. 'She said yes, we went to lunch today.'

'Oh—'

'—I got a call from the city practice about an emergency appointment needing surgery so I...'

There was a pause, and then Esme finished his sentence.

'You left her?'

'Yes. And I forgot to say goodbye.'

'That's how the date ended? Oh, Michael. Why do you always do this?'

Michael frowned.

'Do what? I think I usually manage to say good-bye.'

'You always put work first. Always. And don't say that if she's the right woman, she'll understand. That's not how it works.'

'It was an emergency, Mum.'

'I know.'

'And I'm hiring a head vet so it won't happen

again.'

'Good! That's good. Does Frankie know that?'

'I think I mentioned it.' Michael closed his eyes and ran his hand down his face again. 'Have I screwed it up?' he asked quietly.

'Sweetheart, you're asking the wrong person.'

He sighed and glanced around his quiet office.

'She's a Hollywood movie star, Mum,' he said gently. 'Did her mum mention that? What would she want with me?'

This time Esme sighed down the phone, so softly that Michael almost missed it.

'Esme did mention something about it, I think. I wasn't sure what she meant. Look, Frankie said yes when you asked her out,' his mother told him. 'She went to lunch with you. Sounds like she wants to get to know you. And that's where all this starts, isn't it. Getting to know each other.'

Michael nodded and then gave a 'Yup,' when he remembered his mother couldn't see him.

'Are you going to ask her out again?' Esme asked.

Michael gritted his teeth.

'I am.' Even though she'd probably say no, Michael wanted to give this another chance. 'I'll turn my phone off this time.'

'Good. Ask her when we're done here. Now, I called to ask if we're doing coffee and cake this week?'

'Oh, yes. Of course. Why wouldn't we?'

'Interesting, isn't it,' Esme mused. 'How you

always put work first when it comes to these beautiful, young women, but not with your mother. Not that I'm complaining, not at all. I just wish you could find someone who became such a priority for you.'

Michael held on to those words, even as he arranged a time and place for the coffee and cake with his mother, and they said their goodbyes.

He stared at his phone screen, not blinking, mind whirring.

She was right – of course she was, his mother had a habit of being right – someday a woman would come into his life who would be a priority over his career. He was sure of it. Someone who would understand when he was pulled away by a patient in need, but who he would have to drag himself from.

The memory of leaving his flat, thoughts of Frankie plaguing him as he rushed to the practice, filled his mind. Hadn't he dragged himself away from her? He'd forced himself to leave so hard that he'd forgotten to say goodbye properly. Because he hadn't wanted to say goodbye.

It hardly mattered. She wouldn't want him now. She would reject him this time, he was sure of it.

Yet, his fingers opened his messages and found her name. He typed out a message apologising and asking if she was free for a do-over tomorrow, and then, before he had time to think, he hit send.

She might not want him anymore, but he

absolutely wanted her, and if he didn't ask, he'd never know.

After checking on the cat, who was recovering well, and chatting to the other vet who had performed the surgery, Michael left the practice and went home. Every thought, every mind wander was interrupted by the idea that his phone had beeped. Every time he checked his phone, the screen was blank. There were no notifications, no messages.

For once, Michael was home at a reasonable hour, so he poured himself a glass of wine and fed Agnes. After eating, she climbed into his lap, purring.

'Do you miss me?' he asked, surprised at her sudden affection. 'I'm sorry. It's probably not great that I leave you so much. Maybe I'm not the right home for you.' He stroked along her back and then rubbed her ears as she closed her eyes and leaned into him. 'Should I find you a more loving home?'

Agnes's purring grew louder, her claws kneading into his legs.

Michael laughed.

'Is that my punishment? It's fine, I can take it.' He gave her ears another loving rub and then startled, making Agnes freeze, as his phone beeped.

Fingers trembling with anticipation, he pulled the phone from his pocket. He groaned when he saw Dane's name instead of Frankie's, and opened the message.

Mike! How did the date go? If not well, Rachel really enjoyed last night. She'd love to see you again, but she's scared to message you. Because you haven't messaged her. Could you message her? Don't put me in the middle.

Michael groaned and leaned his head back in the chair. Agnes made herself comfortable and curled up in his lap. After a moment's thought, he messaged Dane back.

Not well. Work pulled me away before we really got started. Don't worry, I'll message Rachel.

He laid his head back again, trying to compose a polite rejection message to Rachel. She'd been lovely – attractive, smart, funny – but he hadn't given her a second thought. It wouldn't be fair on her to suggest otherwise, even if it turned out Frankie wanted nothing more to do with him.

Hi Rachel, it's Michael. It was so lovely to meet you last night. I'm afraid I'm not in the right place for a relationship but maybe I'll see you again at a future event.

Michael reread the message and pulled a face; he

could do better than that. He deleted it and stared at his screen, blowing out his cheeks. His phone beeped and a message from Dane popped up as he fought to find the right words.

That's a shame. What are you saying to Rachel?

Michael sighed and went back to fussing Agnes's ears. She purred, closing her eyes.

I haven't found the right words yet. How do I let her down politely? Are you sure she's interested? It would be easier if she wasn't.

Michael pursed his lips.
'Dear Rachel. You're very lovely but there were no sparks,' he said aloud. Agnes opened one eye to glare at him. 'Well, obviously I can't say that,' he murmured to the cat.

Oh, poor you. Every woman wants you but you're too busy. You'll find the right words.

Michael stared at Dane's reply and frowned.

I didn't ask you to set me up on a blind date. I'm not sure what you were expecting.

He typed out the message and hit send without thinking, heart pounding, and then sat back, breathing hard, regretting his tone a little.

Won't happen again. Promise.

Michael stared at Dane's response. Three dots appeared, suggesting Dane was typing again.

Do you still fancy a drink before Christmas though? Just us. No dates.

Relaxing, Michael smiled.

Of course. Let me know when.

It was only as he hit send that his mother's words came back to him.

'Huh. Turns out I give priority to my friends and my mother.' He frowned, staring down at the cat on his lap. 'So why can't I make a woman a priority? What's wrong with me?'

Agnes didn't reply and Michael went back to staring at his phone.

Hi Rachel. It's Michael. It was lovely to meet you last night but I'm an arse who always puts work first so I can't possibly have a relationship with you. All the best for the future.

Michael immediately deleted the message. As his phone beeped again, he lazily glanced at the screen, expecting a reply from Dane. At the sight of Frankie's name, his eyes widened and he sat up, ignoring Agnes's groan of displeasure.

Please don't worry. I understand that emergencies come up, especially in your line of work. I'd love to try again. Where will you be tomorrow?

Heart in his throat, Michael slowed his breathing and read the message another four times, a smile growing on his lips. He exhaled in a rush and tapped out a reply.

I'll be in Bekburn by lunchtime tomorrow. Shall we meet at the pub at 12pm?

He stared at the phone, waiting for those three little dots. A small noise escaped him as they appeared.

Not sure I can do another pub lunch. How about the coffee shop down the other end of the high street? Shall I meet you outside the practice?

Smiling, nodding to himself, Michael sent a message to agree, telling Frankie he looked forward to seeing her tomorrow. Then he collapsed back into his chair, grinning to himself.

After far too long spent thinking about Frankie

and what tomorrow could bring, Michael lifted his phone and ordered some food to be delivered. Remembering he still hadn't messaged Rachel, he tentatively typed out a polite message before hitting send. He slid Agnes off him and made his way to the bathroom, stripping off his clothes, and was still smiling to himself as he took a hot shower, washing the surgery and day's stress away.

Twenty-Three

If anything, Frankie was more nervous about this second attempt at a first date than she had been about the first date. She'd need a day off at this rate, a whole twenty-four hours spent in front of the TV eating comfort food. Today was Friday, she realised with a jolt, which meant she could actually live that dream the next day, when her house wouldn't be filled with builders.

Her nerves eased a little; even if this date went horribly, she had something to look forward to.

She parked her car off the high street and wrapped her coat tightly around her as she walked towards the practice. The temperature had dropped as the thick layer of grey clouds had lifted, leaving blue sky and a freezing wind behind. Frankie pulled her woolly hat further down over her ears, dug her hands into her pockets and let out a high-pitched 'woo!' as she turned the corner onto the high street, straight into a gust of wind that tried to knock her back.

There, just down the road a little from outside his practice, was the tall figure of Michael. Their eyes met immediately and he gave a nervous smile. She grinned, lengthening her stride and taking care to cross the road.

'Hello,' she said as she approached.

'Hi. I'm so sorry about yesterday.'

'Oh, please. Don't be. I completely understand. Did it all go well?'

Michael nodded, turning so they could walk up the high street towards the coffee shop. He wore a long, dark winter coat with a scarf around his neck, but his head was bare, his ears turning a little pink. Frankie resisted the urge to insist on popping into the craft and gift shop to buy him a hat. Maybe he liked having cold ears.

'It did. A cat had been hit by a car—'

'Oh no!'

'—We had to perform emergency surgery and it required two surgeons, which is why I was called to go.'

'But the cat's okay?'

'He is.' Michael looked down and smiled at Frankie. Heat rushed to her cheeks and she avoided his gaze.

'Good. That's the important thing.'

There was a pause and Frankie became acutely aware that Michael was watching her as they ambled up the high street.

'I'm hiring another vet, a head vet, so hopefully

that won't happen too often anymore.'

Frankie shrugged.

'You'll be called away for emergencies. It's okay. You're a vet, it comes with the job.' She flashed a smile up to Michael and found soft, kind eyes staring back at her. She looked away quickly and swallowed against her dry throat.

'I haven't been to this coffee shop yet,' she managed. 'I hope it's okay.'

'Sandy talks about it sometimes. It always looks cosy.'

'Nice for so close to Christmas,' Frankie murmured, peering in through the steamed-up windows as they approached the door to the coffee shop.

Despite the windows, it wasn't too busy inside. There was a gentle bustle and chatter from the occupied tables. The smell of coffee and cinnamon filled the shop, and Frankie breathed it in.

'Do they do food?' she asked quietly.

'Oh yes, sandwiches and paninis. Maybe soup,' said Michael, leading the way to the queue and the display case of sandwiches on offer. 'What do you fancy?'

Frankie did a double take at Michael and snapped her mouth shut. Now wasn't the time to say she fancied him. She forced herself to read the labels for each sandwich and panini on offer.

'I'll just have the cheese and tomato panini, I think,' she said, stepping forward with the queue.

'Oh, and maybe a muffin,' she added, scouting the cakes further down the line.

Michael smiled.

'What would you like to drink?'

Frankie gave Michael a suspicious, narrowed-eyed look.

'I'm paying,' he told her. 'It's the least I can do after yesterday.'

'But you paid yesterday, on the agreement that I would pay next time. This is next time.'

'True, but this is a do-over, so next time will be the next time. Why don't you go find a table?'

Frankie pulled a face, but Michael's expression became stern. Fighting a smile, Frankie relented.

'Fine. But I'm definitely paying next time, no arguments!'

The straight line of Michael's lips gave way and he smiled again. She wasn't sure which she preferred – obviously the smile, but there was something about that stern look.

'What would you like to drink?' he asked, stepping forward with the queue.

'A bottle of Coke would be good, thanks,' said Frankie, glancing around the coffee shop. 'A table near the back?'

She wandered off as Michael nodded, found a table in the back corner and shrugged off her coat. It was a little darker at the back, but also quieter. The coffee machine and rattle of plates and cups made the front of the shop too noisy. Back here there were a few couples and groups, some quietly chatting, others busy staring at their phones. One man was reading a paper.

It was nice to see the coffee shop so busy on a weekday, considering the size of the town.

There was a small Christmas tree next to the table and Frankie studied the ornaments as she waited. Each one was handcrafted, perhaps by children. Eventually, her gaze found a sign behind the tree explaining that the ornaments had been made by pupils at the local primary school. Smiling to herself, Frankie took off her hat and scarf and considered removing her jumper. It was so warm in there, no wonder the windows were steamed up.

Michael appeared with a tray carrying drinks, plates and a wooden spoon with a number.

'Here we go.' He removed her Coke and a glass and his own coffee, along with plates carrying a chocolate muffin in red and green wrapping and a fancy mince pie, and placed the wooden spoon where it could be easily seen.

'Thank you. A muffin as well!'

'You did mention the muffin. And it gave me an excuse to have a mince pie.'

Frankie gave a soft laugh.

'You must be exhausted, driving between here and Edinburgh so often?' Frankie mused, pouring her Coke into the glass. 'And doing surgery in between!'

'It does get tiring. It's why I've been thinking

about choosing just one place for so long. But it's hard to choose.'

'I know what you mean. I still sometimes wonder if I should have bought somewhere in the city. But look at this!' Frankie gestured to the coffee shop and the little Christmas tree beside them. 'This is so lovely. Plus, you probably wouldn't be my local vet if I'd bought somewhere in the city. We might not have met.'

Michael hesitated.

'Do you think so? Because I think I've seen you more in the city than around here.'

Frankie gave this some thought.

'Oh, you're right.' She met Michael's eyes. 'What do you think that means?'

Her stomach fluttered as his eyes softened. He opened his mouth to respond but was interrupted by their food arriving. They thanked the man who brought the plates and then stayed silent as he took the spoon with their number and vanished back towards the front of the shop.

'So, you'll have more time once you've hired your head vet?' Frankie asked as they began to eat. 'I guess that'll be after Christmas now?'

Michael nodded.

'I'm not even sure we'll get to the interviews before Christmas at this rate.' He sighed. 'I don't like doing interviews.'

'Why not?'

'Everyone's so nervous!'

'Even you?' Frankie laughed.

'Especially me,' said Michael. 'Maybe in the future the head vets I hire can do the interviewing. Although I do like knowing who I'm employing and working with.'

'Of course.'

'But yes, I should have more time. I think,' Michael said slowly, glancing up at Frankie. 'Start the new year right, I guess.'

'What will you do with that extra time?'

'Charity work, I suppose,' Michael said immediately. Then he paused, his panini halfway to his mouth, and looked up at Frankie. 'I should start taking it easier, really. That whole settling down thing that people do.'

'I've been told I should do that, too.' Frankie gave Michael a quizzical look. 'Is settling down what you really want?'

Michael seemed to struggle.

'I don't know.'

'What does it mean? For you. What would settling down mean?'

Michael blinked and placed his food back on his plate.

'To meet someone,' he said quietly, glancing up at her.

She smiled, hoping the shadows around them would hide the flush creeping up her neck.

'To work less?'

Michael pulled a face.

'I'm the same,' Frankie said quickly. 'I like being busy.'

'Me too.'

Their eyes met again, and this time no words would come. Frankie attempted to smile, her heart pounding, her mouth becoming dry. Michael smiled back.

'It's possible to be busy and have a successful relationship, isn't it?' he asked gently.

Something twisted inside Frankie.

'I think it's entirely possible to be busy and in love, yes.'

Michael's eyes flashed and Frankie's breath caught.

'Everyone tells me I work too much,' he said carefully.

'Do you think you work too much?'

Michael sighed and the moment was gone. He looked back down to his food and gave this some thought.

'Yes,' he admitted. 'But I'm not sure I want to change that. I want to change the type of work I do, but I...'

'Like being busy,' Frankie finished for him. 'I still think you can make it work. It depends on how much you want it, and the other person, right?'

Her body was on fire when he looked up and seemed to study her, taking all of her in. She cleared her throat and took a gulp of Coke.

'What would you like to do that's different?' she

asked when it became obvious he wasn't going to say anything further.

'I'm not sure. For a while I considered moving to the west coast and training to work with livestock, but I don't want to leave Edinburgh. I enjoy the charity work I do, I'd love to do more around that.'

Frankie smiled, swallowing her mouthful.

'When I quit acting – retired, whatever – my parents told me to let the ideas breathe. That the next step would make itself clear to me.'

Michael looked at her thoughtfully as he chewed. 'And has it?'

Frankie shook her head.

'Nope.'

Michael smiled, and maybe that was even the beginning of a laugh.

'Although my parents keep giving me looks as if it is clear and I just haven't seen it yet. I don't know. I think it's the problem of aiming for something, expecting to get fulfilment out of it once you're there, getting there and feeling nothing. Know what I mean?'

Michael blinked and looked down at the remains of his panini.

'I think I do. But there's always further up to go, isn't there,' he murmured.

'Oh, there are lots of choices. To keep going, to do something completely different, to stop and just enjoy for a while,' said Frankie, finishing her lunch.

Michael stared down at his final bite, his eyes

glazing in thought. Frankie sat back with her drink, eyeing up the chocolate muffin Michael had bought her.

'Did you say you had a brother?' Frankie asked when, again, Michael didn't seem like he was going to respond.

'Hmm. He lives in Australia with his wife.'

'That's nice. Do you ever get to visit him?'

'Not really. We've been out there once, for the wedding. Me and Mum,' Michael clarified. 'And they've been here once, so Mum could meet her grandchildren.'

'That's a shame you can't see them more often.'

'Hmm. It's a long flight.'

'Other side of the world,' Frankie agreed quietly, watching Michael. 'Are you all right?'

He looked up and smiled.

'Oh, yes.'

'It's just you've gone a bit quiet.'

'Sorry. Is there a toilet here? Excuse me a moment.'

Frankie watched as Michael stood and left the table, disappearing in the direction of the coffee shop's customer toilet. She sat back and blew her cheeks out. Was this going well? She couldn't tell.

Twenty-Four

Going to the toilet hadn't been the best excuse, but it was the best Michael could come up with. He didn't want Frankie seeing him checking his phone. It had vibrated in his pocket as they'd been talking, someone had messaged him, and then it started vibrating repeatedly. Someone had called.

It suggested another emergency, but Michael couldn't let it get in the way of this date.

He glanced at himself in the toilet's mirror, catching his own eye. Could he let work get in the way? She seemed very understanding about the whole thing, but the conversation also seemed stuck in their careers and what they were going to be doing in the future. It wasn't a conversation Michael particularly wanted to have. It involved too much thinking, when it seemed as if that was all he'd been doing these past months, for this past year. He was sick of thinking. He wanted to do. He needed action.

The message and missed call were from Lucia.

Holding his breath, he opened the message.

Got a situation. Are you free?

Biting his lower lip, he rang his voicemail and held his phone to his ear.

'Michael, it's Lucia. I know you're probably busy but if you could call me back as soon as you get this, please. Thank you.'

Michael sighed and stared down at his phone. After a moment, he hit the call button and spoke in a low voice.

'Lucia? What's going on?'

'There's been an incident. Robbie was attacked and his dog was injured. Are you available?'

'I'm in Bekburn. Where are they now? Are they being seen to?'

'The vet on duty is busy elsewhere.'

Michael sighed.

'Busy how? Has someone else been attacked?'

'No.'

Michael almost growled down the phone.

'For the love of— Fine. Take Robbie and Edgar to my practice. I'll call them now and let them know to expect you.'

'Thank you, Michael. You're a lifesaver.'

'We'll see about that. Let me know how it goes.' He hung up and immediately called his own city practice. 'It's Michael. Lucia is on her way with one of Vets On Street's patients. They've been attacked.

The dog needs emergency medical care. And the man might too...'

'I'll ask Lucia when she comes in,' said the receptionist. 'No problem, leave it with me. I'll keep you informed, shall I?'

'Yes, please. Let me know if I'm needed. Is it busy there?'

'No, it's quiet. It shouldn't be a problem.'

'Okay, but you'll let me know?'

'Of course.'

Michael hung up and chewed more on his bottom lip, glancing up at his reflection. His instincts were telling him to leave, to go back to the city. What was he doing on a date, in the toilet of a coffee shop, when a poor man and his dog had been attacked and needed emergency care.

His stomach swirling, and without having made a conscious decision, Michael left the toilet and headed back to Frankie.

'I'm sorry about that. I think I need to go.'

'Oh.' Frankie stood. 'Are you feeling okay?'

'Oh, yes. I'm fine. I just had...' Michael stopped himself as he looked up into Frankie's eyes. What was he doing? He couldn't leave her again. His chest ached as Frankie seemed to sag a little.

'You had a call from work?' she ventured.

'I'm so sorry.'

'There's another emergency?'

'There is.'

'Over the road or in the city?'

Michael hesitated.

'In the city.'

'And they need you,' Frankie murmured, nodding to herself.

Again, Michael hesitated, his hand reaching for his coat. They didn't need him. There was a capable vet, who he had employed, at his practice right now who would do a wonderful job of looking after the dog. Both Lucia and his receptionist had said they'd keep him informed. He had no reason to leave. At least, not yet. He could continue the date and then head back to the city afterwards, have Sandy reschedule his afternoon appointments. It would be fine to do that.

He bit his tongue.

'It's okay,' came Frankie's voice. 'If you need to be there then you need to go. Otherwise you might be late. I understand.' But those last two words came out with a quiver.

Michael shuddered as he exhaled. He thought she'd understand, but she didn't. Maybe no woman ever would.

'I'm sorry,' he murmured, lifting up his coat.

'Here.' Frankie wrapped his mince pie in a tissue napkin. 'For the road, I guess.' She offered him a smile but he couldn't return it. He took the mince pie and gave a singular nod.

'I'll call you,' he murmured.

'Let me know how it goes. And drive safe,' said Frankie, hugging herself. Michael took in her posture and then closed his eyes against a wave of dizziness.

Turning, he left the coffee shop and strode up the road, his coat over his arm, wrapped-up mince pie in his hand. He swung into his rural practice, making Sandy jump, and handed her the mince pie.

'Here, you have this.'

'How did it go?' Sandy asked, glancing around him, presumably for a glimpse of Frankie.

'There's been an incident in the city and I'm needed at that practice. Can you please reschedule my afternoon appointments?'

Sandy sighed.

'Okay, will do.'

'Send me an email with the details,' said Michael, pulling on his coat.

'Did the date go well, at least?'

Michael opened his mouth and then snapped it shut.

'Probably not,' he muttered, giving Sandy a wave and leaving, digging his hand into his pocket to find his keys. His scarf trailed from his other pocket and he pulled it free, throwing it onto the passenger seat as he climbed into his car and started the ignition.

This time, he didn't think about Frankie as he travelled to the city practice. His thoughts concentrated on Robbie and his dog, waiting in the city, scared and in pain. Frankie was there, though, at the back of his mind, vanishing into the distance.

Once at the practice he found everything under control. Everything was calm, and Lucia was talking to a police officer and paramedic in the otherwise empty waiting room. Michael approached carefully, until Lucia noticed and introduced him.

'The dog is just having his wounds cleaned but they're not deep. No surgery required after all.'

Relieved, Michael sat beside Robbie and listened to the others talking. Frankie's face floated in front of him, the disappointed lines at her eyes, the drop of her lips, faltering as she tried to hide it.

He asked Robbie how he was and made some small talk until Lucia was finished with the police officer and the paramedic had finished checking Robbie. They left and Michael stood.

'You didn't have to come,' Lucia told him. 'Everything's under control. Someone on your reception rang the police and ambulance as soon as we arrived. The attack was scary, but it could have been a lot worse. Are you all right? You look exhausted.'

'Thank you,' Michael murmured, looking around the waiting room as if seeing it for the first time. 'If I'm not needed, I think I'll take a walk.'

Lucia nodded and turned back to Robbie.

With the attention off him, Michael left the practice and walked far enough away that his colleagues wouldn't be able to see him. Then he stopped, hands in his pockets, and stared up at the blue sky. The wind was sharp, blowing through him and under his scarf. Michael shivered and started walking slowly, his eyes down, not seeing where he went.

He'd done it again, only this time there'd been no good reason for it. The date had been going okay, he thought. Had it? His memory was already beginning to blur and twist.

When he apparently woke from his thoughts, he was on Calton Hill, staring out across the city, eyes narrowed against the wind. The blue sky had vanished behind a wall of grey cloud, threatening to rain over Edinburgh.

Michael blinked and glanced about him. There were tourists taking photos and the odd dog walker. No one seemed to notice that he hadn't been paying attention. He stepped back and found a bench, sitting and taking a deep breath of the bitter wind.

What was he going to do? Something had to change.

He pulled his phone from his pocket and stared at the blank screen for a moment. Then he found the number he wanted, hit call and held the phone to his ear, leaning back to get some shelter from the wind.

'Michael?'

'Yeah, hi. I screwed up.'

Twenty-Five

After Michael abruptly left, Frankie rushed back to her car with her muffin. She sat there longer than she meant to, staring at the muffin, enjoying the solitude, with no one asking her questions. Eventually she drove home, music blaring, avoided her parents' cottage, cursed the presence of the builders, and locked herself away in her bedroom.

She stayed there, going over the date again and again, wondering what she could have done differently and, finally, realising that she hadn't done anything wrong.

Other than be attracted to Michael in the first place.

Her phone beeping pulled her from her thoughts. It was a message from Sandy.

Hey. Are you ok? Michael came in not looking good. Just want to check in.

Frankie stared at the message, strangely distanced from it, wondering if the person holding her phone would respond and, if they did, what words they would use.

In the end, she did respond.

Hi. Thanks. I'm fine.

She clenched her eyes closed and hit send. If this was a film, she thought, a tear would have squeezed from beneath her eyelids as she'd sent the message and dropped her phone on her bed. There had been a time when she'd been able to do that; remember some heartbreak, put herself back there and squeeze out a tear at just the right moment, hoping the director wouldn't call for another take but knowing he would.

It was almost a shock to find that she wasn't crying. Here she was, in the real-life situation, and there were no tears. But then, there was no audience to convey her pain to.

There was no partner to convey her pain to.

Because he had stood and left, strangely quiet, and Frankie had known in the moment that Michael had walked away that he had no intention of seeing her again.

Finally, her eyes began to sting and a sob ripped through her. She held the tears back, not wanting them now. The moment had gone. Not only was she alone with awful taste in men, but her body's reactions had awful timing.

Two hours later, Frankie heard the builders leaving and there came a soft knock at her bedroom door.

'Miss Taylor?'

Frankie made her way over and took a breath, plastering on a smile and opening the door.

'We're going now. I know it's early—'

'It's okay. It's Friday. Thank you for all your work this week. See you Monday?'

The builder gave her a curious look but it lasted only a second.

'Have a good weekend,' he murmured, turning and leaving. Frankie followed him down the stairs and to the front door, giving him a short wave before closing and locking the door. She turned back to her house and wandered into the building site that was her new open-plan kitchen diner.

It was huge, and it was coming along quickly. They'd be ready to fit the kitchen next week, and the orangery extension was almost up. She'd soon have the house to herself, ready to become lost in design choices, paint and tiles. Frankie leaned against the doorframe, hugging herself, trying not to think about what she'd do once these renovations were finished. Even when the kitchen diner was complete, she had to go through every room. Then the garden. Not to mention her parents' cottage. If she got bored, maybe she'd buy a flat in the city and do it up or rent it out. Become one of those landlords she hated.

Frowning, Frankie shook her head and made her way to the living room where her fridge freezer was humming away. She didn't have to think that far ahead. A renovation of this scale, doing most of the work herself, would take her at least a year. She'd know what she wanted to do after a year.

'You said that a year ago,' she mumbled, opening the freezer and pulling out a tub of ice cream. It was chocolate brownie and she'd bought it on a whim. As if some part of her had known what was coming. She found a clean spoon and sat on the floor, her back resting against the sofa, to wait for the ice cream to melt enough for her to start chiselling away at it. Maybe she should call her agent, take up her offers of podcast interviews, write a book, start her own podcast, start her own charity.

Frankie hesitated with the spoon halfway to her mouth, her mind whirring with that idea. A knock at the door broke her thoughts.

Frankie ignored it.

The person knocked again. It couldn't be her parents; they had a key.

After a moment, her phone beeped.

Are you in? I'm at your front door.

Frankie read Sandy's message another two times before relenting and getting up to unlock the front door.

'Hi. I'm sorry for just turning up, and wow this house is big!' Sandy hesitated, remembering herself. 'Are you all right? Your text didn't sound all right.'

Without answering, Frankie turned and walked to the living room, plonking back down on the floor and digging her spoon into her ice cream.

'Help yourself to tea and biscuits,' she said around the mouthful, gesturing to the kettle on the coffee table with her spoon.

'Oh, love.' Sandy took off her coat and scarf, laying them on the arm of the sofa, and then she wiggled down to sit beside Frankie. 'I'm so sorry.'

Frankie shook her head.

'There's nothing to be sorry about. This is just me and what I do. I fall for a man who either has no interest in me or no interest in a relationship. I keep telling myself the next time will be different, but it never is.' Feeling another wave of tears burning at her nose, Frankie shoved a spoon of ice cream into her mouth.

'No, no, this is what Michael does. I should have warned you. Honestly, I didn't think it would get this far. Or maybe that this time would be different...' Sandy drifted off, staring around the room. 'This really is a beautiful house.'

'Thank you.' Frankie sniffed. 'Wait until it's finished. And now that I know I'm going to spend the rest of my life alone, I can focus on making it stunning.'

'You're not going to spend the rest of your life alone,' said Sandy, nudging Frankie gently.

'No, I am. I'm choosing to. No more men.' Frankie met Sandy's eyes. 'I give up.'

'Frankie?'

Both women started at the sound of Irene's voice calling through the house. Frankie hadn't even heard the front door open.

'In here, Mum!' she called, once she'd determined she wasn't going to choke on the ice cream she'd been about to swallow.

'I thought I saw you come home, but you didn't come over. Is everything all right?' Irene appeared at the doorway and gave Sandy a big smile. 'Oh, hello. I'm Irene, Frankie's mum. Have we met before? Oh, Frankie.' Irene caught sight of her daughter. 'What happened?'

'I'm Sandy. I'm the receptionist at the vets. We met when silly Lily did the silly thing,' Sandy explained.

'Oh yes! So lovely to meet you properly, Sandy. And thank you so much for all of that. You know, Frankie was worried she might not make friends, moving the whole length of the UK.'

'Mum!'

'Well, you were. And I told you you'd be fine.' Irene sat in an armchair opposite the sofa. 'The date didn't go well, then?'

Frankie shrugged.

'What happened?' Sandy asked. 'All I know is

that Michael came into the practice looking pale, said there was an emergency, that the date hadn't gone well, and then he left.'

Tears filled Frankie's eyes before she could stop them.

'He said that?' Her voice quivered and Sandy, realising her mistake, looked to Irene with wide eyes.

'Tell us what happened, sweetheart,' said Irene. 'I'll make us all a cuppa, shall I? Sandy? Tea?'

'Yes, please.' Sandy turned to properly face Frankie. 'Tell us everything.'

Frankie shook her head.

'I don't want to.'

'Come on, sweetheart. It'll help. Maybe you missed something? Maybe this Michael is a bad one. How can we help if you don't tell us?' Irene disappeared for a moment with the kettle and returned with it full of water to switch it on. She perched back on the armchair and gave her daughter a kind smile. 'Go on.'

Frankie sighed, staring down into her melting ice cream. She was beginning to feel sick.

'I thought it was going well. We talked about yesterday, about the emergency he had to rush off to, about work. And then he went quiet, made an excuse to go to the toilet, and when he came back he made his excuses and left. Another emergency.' She glanced at Sandy. 'Was there actually an emergency?'

'One of his charity clients was attacked.' Sandy nodded. 'But I spoke to the receptionist at the city practice, she said everything was fine and under control. Michael didn't need to be there really...'

Frankie couldn't take it anymore. She handed the ice cream to her mother and curled up, willing herself to not be sick.

'Hmm. Does he do this often?' Irene asked Sandy, putting the ice cream back in the freezer.

'Honestly, he doesn't go on dates often.'

'Really? Because he was going on a date the other night when he asked me out,' Frankie managed. 'Maybe he does this all the time. Just asks women out and messes them around.'

Irene frowned.

'Did he pay for anything?'

Frankie looked up into her mother's eyes, fighting against the quiver at her chin.

'Mum, he paid for everything.'

Irene sighed.

'Then I don't know,' she murmured. 'But I can find out,' she added quietly, to herself, standing and patting down her pockets.

Frankie's immediate reaction was to ask what she was planning on doing, but she already knew, and somehow the words wouldn't come. She watched in silence as her mother mumbled to herself, pulling out her phone, telling Sandy it was nice to meet her again, before leaving. The front door clicked shut behind her.

Sandy turned back to Frankie.

'What's that about?'

'Well.' Frankie sniffed 'You know how I said I was done with men? And before you came in I was planning on just forgetting about Michael and throwing myself into these renovations.'

'Yeah?'

'Mum is friends with his mum, so best guess is she's going to call Esme and make even more of a mess of this. There'll be no helping me after that.'

Sandy grinned, holding back a laugh.

'You don't know that it'll make more of a mess of it. Michael's the one who's made a mess here.'

Frankie looked Sandy in the eye.

'Come on. What man wants a woman who seemingly got her mum to call his mum about his bad behaviour?'

Sandy couldn't hold back. She burst into laughter and soon Frankie was joining her, her cheeks still wet with tears.

'Serve him right,' said Sandy, finding some kitchen roll in a nearby box and handing Frankie a sheet. 'And don't you worry. You'll do just fine, with or without him. We've got you.' Sandy squeezed Frankie's free hand as Frankie wiped her cheeks. 'Now, are you going to give me a tour or what?'

Twenty-Six

'Wow,' Jamie murmured, giving a low whistle down the phone. 'This girl must be something.'

Michael sighed into the receiver.

'Yes, she is.' He groaned. 'I've ruined everything. Like I always do.'

This time Jamie sighed down the phone.

'Nah, you can fix this.'

'How?'

'Talk to her? But this time, and I'm just going to throw this idea out there, don't rush off to work. Stay with her. How about that?'

Michael considered throwing his phone across the room.

'If only you could have told me that earlier,' he muttered.

Jamie laughed.

'Did I ever tell you how much I screwed up my first date with Kelly?'

'You got drunk and threw up.'

'Yeah, and the next day, I called, apologised, and now we're married with kids. See? Just call her and apologise.'

Michael sighed. If only it were that easy.

'You've got to do it, Mike,' Jamie continued into the silence. 'Mum's met her now.'

A smile hit Michael and he almost laughed.

'True.'

The doorbell buzzing made Michael startle and sit up from where he'd been lying on his back, on his bed, staring up at the ceiling as he talked to his brother. Agnes, who had been asleep curled on his stomach, gave a cry and sprang off the bed.

'Someone's at the door. Best go.'

'Fine. Call her, Mike. Apologise. Explain. Beg. Whatever you have to do. Whatever you're willing to do. Right? Because the right woman is worth fighting for.'

Something shifted inside Michael and he nodded.

'Right. Thanks. Talk to you later.'

'Keep me updated!' Jamie added quickly before they said a hurried goodbye and hung up.

With wobbly legs, Michael went to the intercom.

'Hello?'

'Michael, it's your mother. Open this door, please.'

Frowning, Michael did as he was told and went through his own front door, down the stairs to the building's front door.

Esme hadn't visited Michael since the day after he'd gotten the keys. She'd proclaimed the stairs were too much and that he'd have to come to her from now on. What was she doing here? Maybe she'd sensed that something wasn't right.

The idea of his mother belonging to a coven of witches popped into his head; book-reading, wine-drinking witches. Michael mentally shook the image away as he opened the door to his mother.

She held up a hand and gestured for him to return to his flat. He did so slowly, aware of his mother climbing the stairs behind him in a ragged silence. He turned back to her as he reached his own front door.

'Mum, what—'

'No! No.' Esme held up a hand, out of breath. 'I'm talking. I just... I'm going to sit down first.'

Michael closed the front door behind her as she wandered into the living room and sat in an armchair. Agnes was immediately on her lap. 'Oh, Agnes, it's been so long.' Esme rubbed the cat's ears and Agnes purred, shooting Michael a look.

'Okay. Would you like a cup of tea?'

'Please,' said Esme, fussing over Agnes.

Michael disappeared into the kitchen and paused. What was his mother doing here? She certainly wasn't happy. He put the kettle on and reached for a clean mug and a tea bag. Could she know about the date? How could she possibly know about the date?

Michael froze.

Frankie's mother was friends with his mother.

Frankie would have told her mother, because that's what women did, wasn't it. He closed his eyes and took a deep breath. At least now he would be prepared.

He took two cups of tea out into the living room and then brought out a plate of biscuits. Agnes showed them some attention until Esme told her off and Agnes relaxed back into her lap.

Esme had caught her breath and she stared at her son until Michael began to wilt.

'Mum—'

'No, I'm doing the talking. You just sit there and listen, until I ask you a question.'

Michael sighed and clasped his hands in his lap, waiting.

Esme pursed her lips and looked around the room, stopping when she saw the piano.

'You're still playing?'

Michael nodded.

'Every morning,' he said carefully, wondering if speaking would warrant a telling off.

Esme gave a nod of approval.

'I miss hearing you play.'

'I can play for you now?'

'No, I'm angry with you. You can play for me later.'

Michael leaned forward.

'Why are you angry with me, Mum? Is this about—'

'The poor girl,' said Esme, lifting her cup of tea to

her lips and blowing on it. 'I thought you wanted to make changes in your life.'

'I do—'

'Then why did you leave her like that? And don't give me that emergency rubbish. Your receptionists talk, you know. We know you didn't have to rush back to the city. So why did you?'

Michael went to answer but his mother cut him off.

'Don't you think you should be telling Frankie, not me?'

Michael closed his mouth and gave his mother a look.

'Do you want to see her again?' Esme asked, not giving him a chance to respond.

'Of course,' he said without thinking, catching himself off guard.

Esme watched, a smile sneaking onto her lips.

'You didn't think you did, did you. You'd written it all off, hadn't you.'

Michael went back to looking down at his clasped hands.

'What happened, Michael?' Esme breathed, sitting back, stroking Agnes.

'I don't know,' Michael murmured, still staring at his hands. 'It was going well and then... I felt my phone ringing in my pocket, and I couldn't... I couldn't leave her again. But what if I was needed? And she said she understood about emergencies. And then it became a bit of a blur, and...'

'And?'

Michael looked up at his mother.

'What if I neglect her? What if I let her down? What if she leaves me?'

'Why on earth would she leave you?'

'Because...' Michael stopped, his eyes burning. 'Because that's what my girlfriends do. Ever since I was a teenager.'

After a few moments of silence, Michael looked up to find his mother watching him with soft eyes.

'You can't think like that,' she told him gently. 'Not every girl has left you.' She rubbed Agnes's ears thoughtfully. 'You never worried about them leaving you, though, before the relationship started?'

Michael frowned.

'No. I don't think so.'

'Did you ever give it much thought?'

With a sigh, Michael sat back.

'I don't remember, which probably means no.'

'But you have this time. Why is that? Because you want your life to be different? Or because Frankie is different?'

Michael stared past his mother, lost in his thoughts.

'I've never felt this way about a woman, and I hardly know her. That's ridiculous, isn't it? I kept seeing her everywhere I went and I kept hoping I'd see her. She has the most beautiful smile. I just want to keep making her smile.'

'You should tell her that,' came his mother's soft voice.

'I can't make her smile if I'm always rushing away because of work.'

The clink of Esme putting her cup of tea down on the coaster brought Michael back to the room.

'You've been such a good boy,' she told him. 'Ever since you were a child. You've studied and worked hard. You've done your father proud. I think it's time for you to step back.'

'I am doing, I just—'

'I know you're planning on taking that step back, but are you really? You're hiring more staff, and that's a good thing, but only because you now have two practices forty-five minutes apart and you've finally learned you can't be in two places at once when it comes to work. That applies to life, in general. For so long, work has been your priority, and I truly believe it's because there was nothing else in your life worthy of being a top priority.'

'You're a top priority, Mum.'

Esme waved his words away.

'Is it at all possible that you've met someone who could be a top priority?'

Michael swallowed hard.

'It is.'

'And are you really going to just give up and let her go without a fight, because you did something stupid that can be easily fixed?'

'Can it be easily fixed?'

'Of course it can! Make a gesture, apologise, show her what she means to you now and what she could mean to you in the future.'

Michael blinked, glancing down to Agnes. He hadn't given the future much consideration. Since he'd met Frankie, he'd just been overwhelmed with the urge to be near her. A proper kiss at the end of the date would have been a success. A future was something else entirely, but as the idea seeped into his mind, painting pictures, it didn't seem like such a bad thing.

'I don't think she'd give me a third chance,' he murmured, still lost in what could be.

'Third time's the charm,' said Esme. 'Now, call her and apologise.'

Michael focused on his mother.

'How did you know what happened?' He reached for his untouched tea, going cold.

'Irene called me. Frankie was very upset. Her mother wanted to know what happened, if there was any reason for it.'

A shiver went through Michael and he put his tea down without drinking any, his stomach turning.

'What did you tell her?'

'That you're an idiot who hasn't figured it out yet, but that you will.' Esme glanced at the piano. 'Play me some music while I eat these biscuits and then I'll leave you to call Frankie. Deal?'

Michael smiled. That didn't sound like much of a deal.

'I can take you home, Mum.'

'No. I'll be fine. You're to call Frankie, and then call me and let me know how it goes. But first, play for me.'

Wordlessly, Michael moved over to the piano, his fingers hovering over the keys, remembering Frankie reaching out to the piano, the ghost of her presence beside him. Closing his eyes, he began to play. Not a jazz tune, but something more classical that he knew his mother loved.

The flat filled with the gentle music, and when he'd finished, he looked over to his mother to find both her and Agnes with their eyes closed.

Smiling, he waited for Esme to open her eyes and look to him.

'That was beautiful. I'm so glad you've kept it up. Does Frankie know you play?'

'She does.'

'Call her. Now. I'll be on my way.' Esme gently pushed Agnes off her lap and picked up the remaining biscuits, wrapping them in a tissue from her pocket. 'Don't you worry about me, but call me when you've spoken to her. All right?'

'All right, Mum.' Michael followed Esme to the front door. 'Thank you.'

'She'll be a lucky girl,' Esme told him, turning to give him a look over. 'Whoever you decide you want to be with.'

Michael gave a nod, not quite agreeing with her. Esme took his hand, squeezed it and then left.

After watching her disappearing down the stairs, Michael closed the front door and nearly tripped over Agnes as he returned to the living room. Standing by the window, he watched his mother walk down the road, nibbling a biscuit from her pocket, and he pulled out his phone.

After three rings, he was sure Frankie wasn't going to answer. Then, on the sixth ring, she picked up.

'Hi.'

'Hi,' he managed, his chest aching at the tone of her voice. 'I'm so incredibly sorry,' he said before he had time to think. 'I'm an idiot.'

'You're not an idiot.'

'I am, but please, let me explain.' Michael sat on his piano stool. 'I have an awful habit of doing this. My priority has always been work. And this is the first time I've... You're the first woman I've met who I've wanted to make a priority. And I think that... scared me.' He swallowed. 'I understand if I've ruined this, but I really like you. I think there could be something here. And I promise I won't do that again. I won't just abandon you like that ever again.'

He stopped when there came a soft laugh down the phone.

'Don't make promises you can't keep,' said Frankie. 'I know sometimes there will be emergencies and you'll have to rush off. It's the nature of the job. It's just hard to see a future when we can't even get started.'

'We can get started,' said Michael a little too quickly. 'I won't ruin it next time. I can promise that.'

There was a pause and Michael could only hope Frankie was smiling.

'You're thinking of a future?' he asked quietly when she didn't say anything.

Her laugh was stronger this time.

'Always. I just thought you didn't want to be in mine,' she told him. 'Are you still scared?'

'Not as much as I was,' Michael admitted.

'What changed?'

'I can't tell you.'

'Why not?'

'Because if I tell you my mum talked it through with me, you might think less of me.'

This time Frankie's laugh was loud.

'I'd think more of you. I think more of you,' she corrected. 'Every day,' she added, sending a rush of warmth through Michael.

'Will you give me another chance?'

Frankie sighed down the phone.

'Of course I will. Come and pick me up, that way you can't abandon me. Tomorrow, six o'clock. Are you free then?'

'I am,' said Michael, mentally moving some appointments. 'I'll pick you up at six.'

'Knock on the farmhouse door,' said Frankie. 'See you at six.'

Twenty-Seven

At two minutes to six, Michael pulled into the farmhouse's drive and parked up. Frankie watched secretly from the window as he glanced at the cottage to his right and then walked straight to the farmhouse's front door. There was a pause, and then he knocked.

Frankie took a deep breath. He had come, which was a start. He was even a little early, which was nice. Would he stay? Frankie's chest tightened at the thought of him leaving for some emergency again. He wouldn't, though, not this time. Surely.

She hadn't made enough of an effort, considering this was potentially a third date, or the third take of a first date. Twice she'd dressed up for Michael, and this time she just couldn't bring herself to do it. Instead, she'd left on her paint-splattered dungarees over a black t-shirt, but she'd let her hair down.

Michael exhaled in a rush as she opened the front door. His tall frame filled the doorway. There were jeans beneath his long coat, although she couldn't see much else. She gave a nervous smile and stepped aside to let him in.

'Hi. Come on in.'

Michael stepped inside and looked around. How much did he remember of the farmhouse when it had been for sale? Frankie knew he'd viewed it, but had he pored over the photographs in the same way she had? Without the builders filling it with their presence and noise, the house was almost silent, and large.

'You've opened it up,' Michael breathed.

'I have. Do you want to see? You can leave your coat there, don't worry about your shoes. It's all a work in progress,' said Frankie, disappearing into the kitchen as Michael removed his coat and scarf, revealing a Christmas jumper beneath.

'You got the heating working?' he asked as he stepped through into what had once been a narrow and dark kitchen. Now the new large room was filled with gentle light from low overhead bulbs in the kitchen and a couple of floor lamps. Although Frankie wanted to show off the beginnings of new kitchen cabinets, his eye was caught by the outline of the garden and shadows of hills beyond through the new orangery extension.

'Wow.'

'Do you like it? The orangery isn't quite finished. I've always wanted an orangery. I mean, it won't be used for oranges, it'll just be a sunroom where I can eat breakfast and maybe do some work.'

'Work?'

'Yeah. If what I decide to do involves the use of a laptop or a table.' Frankie grinned, looking around at the work done. 'And this will be a big kitchen diner, of course. The kitchen pretty much where it was before, but all opened up. A large, country-style table here.' Frankie walked into the middle of what used to be the dining room, arms spread wide. 'The flooring is going in the week after next, I think. I hope. It's all happening really quick but also, I'm so sick of it all.' She laughed and then caught sight of Michael's expression, remembered herself and quietened. 'I'm glad you like it.'

'I would never have thought to have done this,' said Michael, watching her.

'This is only the start, really. It's probably why I'm already fed up.' Frankie moved back to the doorway and gestured for him to follow. 'The staircase is staying, as it's original but safe. There will be all new flooring. The bathroom at the back will be redone eventually. Here's the living room—' Frankie gestured into the room where most of the kitchen appliances were arranged on two coffee tables, surrounded by boxes, an armchair, a sofa and a big American-style fridge freezer. 'And I'm not sure what to do with this room.'

He followed her to the end of the hallway and smiled at the small room, currently empty except for a few boxes that were overspill from the living room.

'Ah, well, this is my study.' His snapped his mouth shut and Frankie looked up at him, her stomach flipping. Avoiding Frankie's gaze, he cleared his throat and stepped into the room. 'I mean, I think many families would use it as a snug. Or something.'

'I did consider making it a snug,' came Frankie's careful voice. 'But then I wouldn't use the living room. It's the problem, I guess, with it just being me.' She trailed off a little, enough that Michael glanced at her, allowing her to catch his eye and hold it. Frankie smiled and stepped closer. 'You'd make this your study, huh?' she breathed.

Michael watched her lips.

'I would.'

'Maybe with French doors leading onto the patio,' Frankie suggested, moving closer.

Michael inhaled sharply.

'That sounds wonderful.'

Frankie stopped once she was right in front of him, gazing up into his eyes, glancing at his lips.

'I'm so sorry about everything,' Michael murmured.

Frankie smiled, her breath catching as her mind whirred with possibilities.

'You're not leaving again, are you?'

'Absolutely not,' he whispered, leaning down to kiss her.

Just before their lips met, there came a knock at

the front door and they jumped apart. Heart pounding, Frankie looked away, back into the hallway as visions of a desk and computer facing the French doors vanished back into the old-fashioned, wallpapered room with bare floor and normal window with its view of the hills and the low hanging branches of a nearby tree.

Michael was staring around the empty room, so Frankie left him to stride back to the front door, muttering, 'Who could that be?' She glanced through the peephole and sighed. 'Mum! What's up?'

'I just wondered if your friend was free for a moment?' said Irene, peering into the house.

Michael followed Frankie and appeared behind her.

'Hello, Mrs Taylor.'

'Oh, please, it's Irene. It's nice to meet you, Michael, under nicer, less rushed circumstances. I've heard a lot about you.' She reached out a hand and Michael took it to shake.

'Yes, so my mother tells me.' He glanced at Frankie. 'I'm very sorry to have upset your daughter.'

'He's apologised a lot, Mum, and now every-thing's fine. So...' Frankie gave her mother a not-so-subtle look, but Irene ignored her.

'I know this is very naughty of me, but we never did book a proper follow-up appointment for Lily, and...' Irene tailed off, giving Michael a hopeful look.

He brightened and gave Irene a smile.

'Of course! Are you worried about her?'

'Oh, no. No. Not really. It's just, she was blinking a lot and we wondered if she'd managed to poke herself in the eye or something.'

'No problem,' said Michael, stepping around Frankie, letting a hand linger on the small of her back as he went. A shiver of pleasure ran up her body and she almost fell forward when his hand left her.

'No, no,' said Frankie, putting out an arm to stop him. 'You can't take advantage of him like that, Mum. We can book an appointment, do everything above board.'

'It really is no problem,' Michael assured her. 'It won't take a moment to look at Lily's eyes.' He turned back to Irene, gesturing for her to lead the way.

Frankie followed, hugging herself, as Irene took Michael to the cottage, into the kitchen where Geoff was drinking a cup of tea and Lily was in her bed. The cottage was warm, the low sound of the radio playing filled the hallway and kitchen, and the smell of fresh mince pies seeped through the house.

'Have you been baking?' Michael asked.

Lily, tail thumping, jumped up at the sound of his voice and gave a sharp bark.

'Yes, mince pies! They're almost ready. Michael here is just going to look at your eyes,' Irene told the dog. 'It's nothing to worry about.' She flashed her husband a smile.

'Oh, you don't need to do that,' Geoff told Michael. 'She's fine. I'm sorry, ignore Irene. You're on a, erm, date with Frankie.' He glanced back to Frankie, standing behind Michael. She gave an exaggerated shrug, eyes wide, but he only shrugged back; there wasn't much else he could do.

'It really is no problem, and it's a pleasure to finally meet you both properly. Hello, Lily.' Michael crouched and opened his arms to the dog. Cautiously, Lily made her way over and sniffed him. Michael gently patted his pockets. 'Oh, I'm afraid my dog treats are in my coat back in the farm-house.'

'Oh, here.' Geoff reached into his pocket and pulled out a bag of treats. 'Forgot to take these out after our morning walk.' He handed Michael the bag.

'Thanks. What do I have here, Lily?' Michael offered Lily a few of the treats and Lily happily crunched them, letting Michael get closer. Stroking her head and ears, Michael crouched lower to look into her eyes. Once she'd swallowed, he put a hand under her chin and lifted her head to study her further. Lily glanced beyond him, wagging her tail at Frankie as she blew a kiss to the dog.

'She's fine,' said Michael. 'Although the eye is a little bit red, there's nothing in there. I can pop round some eye drops, to help it heal. Is she good at letting you put drops in?'

Geoff barked a laugh.

'Nope. Not even for a bit of chicken or sausage. That would be good of you.'

'See, I told you her eye was still red,' Irene said. 'Thank you, Michael. That would be wonderful of you, and of course, let us know how much we'd owe you.'

'Oh, don't worry about that.'

'Can I take Michael back now?' Frankie asked her mother.

Irene pulled on oven gloves and removed a tray of mince pies from the oven.

'You may. And take some of these with you.'

'There won't be any left for us!' said Geoff.

'I'll make more,' Irene told him, putting the mince pies carefully onto a plate and passing the plate to Frankie.

Frankie herded Michael out of the cottage and across the drive, back to the farmhouse.

'I'm so sorry about that.'

'Don't be! It's nice to finally meet your parents, and always nice to see Lily. Especially when she's looking so well. It's nice she still likes me. Hopefully your parents like me too.'

Frankie closed the front door behind them, blocking out the cold, and led Michael into the living room.

'You want my parents to like you?' she asked, placing the plate on the coffee table, next to the kettle.

'Of course,' said Michael before stopping.

'Because they're clients,' said Frankie.

Michael stopped, and Frankie watched a flash of panic cross his eyes until she gave him a sheepish smile. She approached him, standing a little closer than she had to, looking up into his eyes.

'Because they're your parents,' he told her, leaning down.

Frankie's stomach flipped, and although it was pleasurable, a wave of panic swept over her at what was about to happen. Her eye twitched, becoming itchy.

'Would you like a mince pie?' she asked, moving away.

Michael pressed his lips together and sat on the sofa.

'They do smell good,' he said, watching Frankie put the kettle on. She sat beside him, rubbed at her eye and then chuckled to herself.

'This happened last time Lily needed eye drops. My eye got itchy. I was worried I caught something from her.' She rubbed her eye again.

'You'll make it worse if you keep rubbing at it.'

'It's itchy,' said Frankie, sighing. 'Maybe something got into it when we were walking back over.' She blinked furiously.

'Here.' Michael moved so he could look into Frankie's eye and she stayed still, opening her eye wide. 'There's nothing there. Just try to ignore it,' he murmured as his focus moved from checking one eye to looking into both. Her heart pounded as he leaned forward again and, before anything else could interrupt them, pressed his lips against hers.

His warmth spread through her and she stopped for a moment, worried that if she moved, he'd break the kiss. When he didn't, she leaned into him, lifting a hand to brush her fingers up his shoulder and across the back of his neck. He deepened the kiss, snaking an arm around her waist to ease her closer.

The kettle clicked off, but they both ignored it. Frankie wrapped her arms around him, her fingers in his hair as heat rushed through her body. She shuffled closer to him on the sofa, but it wasn't enough. His hands were on the small of her back. She wanted them all over her.

Eventually, it was Frankie who broke the kiss.

Breathing hard, she looked up into Michael's soft eyes.

'I haven't shown you upstairs,' she murmured, kissing Michael's lips quickly. 'Would you like to see the bedrooms?'

Michael nodded, standing hastily. Frankie followed suit, taking his hand and rushing to the stairs. He raced her up to the landing and she led him straight into her bedroom. Smiling, he looked around.

'It's very nice, I like what you've done with it.'

Frankie laughed.

'I haven't done anything yet.'

He let go of her hand and she unclipped her dungarees, turning when she realised Michael had moved.

'Is this my number on your wall?'

Frankie hesitated. Damn.

'Yes?'

'On the Post-it note I gave you, when Lily ate something she shouldn't have.'

'Hmm.'

Michael looked back to her.

'You put it on your wall?'

Frankie pulled her t-shirt over her head and faced Michael.

'I was going to message you, to ask you out, but I couldn't work up the nerve.'

Michael's eyes had strayed down her body. He straightened and walked over to her, wrapping his arms around her waist again. Frankie shivered as his fingers touched her bare skin, and she wiggled out of her dungarees, letting them fall to the floor.

Michael bent to kiss her lips, stopping only as she pulled his Christmas jumper and then the t-shirt beneath over his head. She led him to the bed.

'Do you want to?' she asked, belatedly.

Michael gave a quick laugh and sat beside her, running a finger over her bare shoulder and bra strap.

'Absolutely. Do you?'

Frankie grinned and moved to straddle him.

'More than anything,' she whispered in his ear as she pulled at his jeans.

Michael took her hands, slowing things down, kissing her lips as he unclasped her bra.

She wrapped herself about him, pressing her skin against his as she kissed him hard, leaving the cold of December behind.

Twenty-Eight

Three hours passed in a whirlwind. Michael lay next to Frankie, her head on his chest, his fingers stroking her back and naked hip.

'Are you hungry?' came her muffled voice.

'I could eat.' Michael bent his head to kiss her hair and then watched, not hiding his smile, as she sat up and started looking for clothes. 'What are you doing?' he asked her naked body.

She turned and caught him staring. Grinning, she threw her bra at him and pulled on her t-shirt and dungarees without underwear.

'I'm going to look for food, see what I've got.'

'What about your mum's mince pies?'

'Oh yeah! I forgot about them.' Frankie gave Michael a calculating look and then shook her head. 'Nope. Not on the bed. I don't mind a naked man in my bed, but I can't cope with crumbs. Come on, we're going downstairs.'

Michael groaned as he pushed up from the bed and found his underwear and jeans. Pulling on his t-shirt and grabbing his jumper, he followed Frankie downstairs.

It was hard to concentrate when she was bustling around the living room without underwear on. Not that you could really tell, unless you looked closely, but Michael knew. He'd seen it.

She caught him staring and grinning again.

'What?' she asked, smiling.

'Nothing. Just...happy.' His smile faltered. 'Could we have done this sooner if I hadn't panicked each time?'

'Is that what that was? You weren't just being married to your job?' said Frankie, putting on the kettle and handing Michael a mince pie. He sat on the sofa and Frankie cosied up beside him.

'Well, that too,' Michael murmured, gazing down at her dungarees.

'Do you want me to go put some underwear on?' she whispered. 'Will that help?'

'Absolutely not.' He shook his head and his breath caught as Frankie leaned in and kissed him. He held her close, prolonging the kiss, until the kettle clicked off.

She made the cups of tea and helped herself to a mince pie. For a while, they ate in silence, Michael sat properly and Frankie sat on one leg, her other foot moving up and down his jeans leg, pulling up the fabric. Sex with Frankie was everything he had dreamed of. The smell of her, the taste of her, the feel of her soft skin against his. Only the reality was so much sweeter. He couldn't imagine ever tiring of it.

'These are amazing,' said Michael, finishing his mince pie quicker than he meant to. He waited impatiently for Frankie to finish hers, sipping at his scalding tea and failing to ignore the warm shivers that swept through him every time her toes touched his skin.

'They are. You'll be sad to know I haven't inherited my mum's baking skills.'

'That's okay,' said Michael, wrapping his arms around her as she swallowed the last of the mince pie. He kissed her neck, pushing her hair away, and Frankie relaxed back with a sigh. Michael unclipped one of her dungaree straps and found a breast over her t-shirt as he planted soft kisses down to her collar bone.

'Really? Again?' Frankie asked with a laugh.

'You don't want to?' Michael looked up into her eyes and she smiled down at him.

'Of course I do. I just... Where was this Michael when I first wanted him?'

'That Michael was an idiot.' He pressed his lips against hers and then hesitated. 'When did you first want me?'

'The moment I laid eyes on you,' said Frankie, pulling him closer, kissing him hard.

Michael smiled and broke the kiss.

'I wanted you the moment I met you. Actually, a little before. My mum did a love spell...'

Frankie gave him a look.

'You know, my mum mentioned something about that. It wasn't for us, though?'

'It was for me. To find someone. And I dreamed of the most beautiful woman, and then I met you. And it was you I'd dreamed of. And then I kept seeing you. And dreaming about you.' Michael went back to kissing her neck, his hand finding the bottom of her t-shirt and sliding up against her warm skin. She melted a little as his fingers found her bare breasts.

'You dreamt about me?' she breathed.

Michael nodded, and unclipped the other dungaree strap, pushing up her t-shirt.

'Had you seen any of my films?' came Frankie's voice. 'Or TV shows?'

'No. I'd never seen you before in my life.'

'That's weird.'

'Very.' Michael's lips found her nipple and Frankie inhaled sharply, arching her back in response. It drove him on, his tongue circling her nipple, desperate to hear her moan.

'Is that why you panicked and ran away? Was there even a work emergency?'

Her fingers were in his hair, but still the words made him stop and back off. Frankie blinked, focusing on him, her chest heaving.

'There were work emergencies,' Michael told her. 'But I know I was scared. Dreaming of you, it was a little...intense. The first time was a real emergency, but that second one…' He sat back and Frankie gave a pained look, which he noted but didn't act on. 'I've been talking for so long about things needing to change, but I wasn't really doing anything about it. Hiring more people is something, but I'm not sure it would have made any difference.'

'It wouldn't?' Frankie looked up from Michael's clothed chest to his eyes.

'I would have made excuses, just like I did when I left you on those dates.' He met her gaze sheepishly. 'I'm an idiot,' he added quietly.

'Not an idiot. You were scared. I understand that. If I met a stranger I'd dreamt about, I'd be scared too. Never mind the rest of it,' Frankie told him gently, running her fingers over his hair and brushing them against the back of his neck. 'It's okay. Look, consider this the new beginning, yeah?'

Michael gave a defiant nod.

'Yes. This is the new beginning. Things have to change, and this time I really will make those changes.' He moved forward, scooping Frankie into his arms and kissing her lips as she grinned. 'You're my new priority,' he told her, bumping his nose against hers.

Frankie laughed.

'Okay, easy. Let's just take it as it comes. You're passionate about your work and I don't want to get in the way of that.'

'But I don't want the work to get in the way of us

ever again,' Michael told her.

She kissed him.

'Then it won't. We can make it work, if that's what you want.'

Michael, heart pounding, gazed down at her ruffled clothes and then back up to her beautiful eyes, and nodded.

'More than anything.'

'I don't think that's your brain talking,' said Frankie playfully, sliding a hand down to his crotch.

'It's my heart,' Michael said huskily as his body responded to her touch and he pushed his hands beneath her clothes to wrap around her waist. He buried his head in her neck, breathing her in.

'We'll take it slow,' she repeated. 'Figure it out as we go.' She pushed her fingers through his hair.

'Any day you could wake up and realise you can do better.' Michael hadn't meant to say that, but his brain wasn't working on a full blood supply anymore. The words had slipped out, as easily as his hands slipped back up to her breasts.

He froze, waiting for her response.

Without hesitating, Frankie laughed.

'Don't be ridiculous. I've looked, and there is no better. I just want you.'

Michael lifted his head to search her eyes and she gazed back, stroking his cheek. She leaned forward and gave him a soft, tender kiss.

The kiss turned harder, deeper, and Frankie pushed Michael back to climb on him. Straddling his legs, she pulled off her t-shirt and leaned down to kiss his neck.

Stunned, Michael ran his fingers down her bare back.

'The new hires will help at work,' he murmured to himself. 'And I can dedicate more time to the Bekburn practice, to be closer to you.'

Frankie made a negative noise and lifted her head.

'No, I like coming into the city. You can split your time however you like. And anyway, if you do that, you won't be able to do the charity work. And you said you enjoy that.'

'I do,' said Michael, his gaze dropping.

Smiling, Frankie took his hands and placed them on her breasts.

'We can discuss schedules later,' she told him.

He nodded, preoccupied.

'Would you want to do more charity work?' Frankie asked.

Michael leaned forward and brushed his lips over her nipple, playing with it thoughtfully.

'I would.' He sat back and looked up into her eyes. A jolt of pleasure rushed through him at the sight of her expression. 'I'd like to do more for the homeless. More than free veterinary care.'

'Like what?' Frankie ran her fingers down Michael's jumper and then pulled it and the t-shirt gently over his head. He moved forward, letting her work, trying to arrange his thoughts. They should be having this conversation without the sex, but Michael had a feeling it would take a while before they could keep their hands off each other for long enough.

'Like a hostel. Or those big apartment blocks being built everywhere.'

'The purpose-built ones with gyms and things?'

Michael nodded and Frankie kissed his lips, pushing her bare chest against his. He held her close for as long as she allowed, until she pulled away.

'Nicer than a hostel.'

'Hmm.' Frankie dropped her dungarees to the floor and climbed back onto him.

'Shouldn't we go upstairs?' he murmured, swallowing hard at the sight of her.

'In a minute.' She kissed his lips, his chin, his chest, his stomach, and then stopped. Michael groaned as she moved back up to his lips. 'I've been wondering what to do with my money,' she said.

'Hmm. What?' Michael blinked, his hands on her thighs, willing her into position.

'I have all this money from the films I made. I've been saving it for whatever came next, but I have no idea what that is. I love property—'

'Property developer.' Michael nodded. 'That's what you should do.' His fingers began exploring between her legs.

Frankie's breath audibly caught and she moaned into his lips, kissing him gently.

'But I always feel guilty,' she breathed. 'When there are people who need that housing more than me. I've been thinking a lot lately, and I've been chatting with a housing charity that – oh—'

'That?' Michael removed his hands, placing them on her back and she gave him a dangerous look.

'We should go upstairs,' she told him. 'If you feel more comfortable there?'

'No, no. Hang on. What about this housing charity?'

Frankie groaned and the frustration only made Michael smile, his whole body aching for her.

'I've been talking to a housing charity about investing in some property that I can rent out at a low rate to the charity to give people homes.'

Michael stopped, staring past Frankie.

'That's a great idea,' he said. 'Maybe I could help with that.'

'I'm not sure how. Unless you want to invest in properties as well, and I'll do them up.' Frankie gave the smallest of shrugs and ran her fingers down his chest. His thoughts flickered, but some part of his brain was still working it out. 'Can we talk about this later?' she asked, her hands reaching his groin.

Inhaling, Michael nodded.

'Later,' he murmured, pulling her in for a kiss and moving his hands back between her legs. She grinned against his lips as she undid his jeans and reached inside.

They didn't make it upstairs, which Michael didn't mind. He sat on her sofa and she still sat on him, splayed, her head back on his chest.

'I can hear your heart beating,' she murmured.

'I'd be worried if you couldn't.' Michael glanced around the room, hoping her parents over in their cottage were none the wiser about what he'd been doing to their daughter. 'You don't have any Christmas decorations up yet.'

'You're only noticing that now?'

'I noticed it earlier, but I was distracted.'

Frankie laughed and kissed his chest without moving.

'I wanted to wait until the builders were done but it's taking longer than I thought it would. Do you want to come and help me choose a tree?' she asked, lifting her head.

'If you'd like me there.' Michael ran a hand down the side of her body.

'Well, I'm buying a few. There's already one outside the house, and then one for my parents – but they're choosing that one – and one for in here. Do you have one for your flat?'

'Only an old, plastic secondhand one.'

Frankie pulled a face.

'Then we should go buy you a tree. A real one. Where do you buy a Christmas tree in the city?'

Michael smiled, watching her.

'I'll figure it out,' he murmured, brushing her

long hair from her shoulder, just as he had before they'd met, while he'd been sleeping.

Frankie stopped and smiled.

'This is nice, isn't it,' she said.

'I could get used to it,' he told her, reaching for his cup of tea before remembering it would be cold.

'Me too,' said Frankie, resting back against him. 'We'll figure it all out, won't we?'

'We will,' Michael assured her, lifting her fingers to his lips. 'I wonder what Agnes will make of it all.'

Frankie laughed.

'I think she might like a farmhouse surrounded by fields.'

Michael's eyes softened as he looked down at the woman from his dreams.

'I think I'd like the woman who owns the farm-house.'

Frankie laughed.

'You got her,' she whispered, before wrapping her arms around his neck and kissing him.

A YEAR LATER

'We don't have time for this.'

'It won't take a moment,' Frankie told her mother, picking up her skirts and jogging through the farmhouse. The kitchen diner had been completed, along with the orangery, almost a year ago. The living room was now cosy and comfortable with a large sofa surrounding a fireplace and TV. Upstairs, the bedrooms were finished with new floorings, new plaster and paint on the walls and beds ready for guests coming to stay. All except the small back bedroom, which Frankie had kitted out with a desk and bookshelves, for when she wanted to work on the screenplay her agent had finally talked her into writing. She didn't have high hopes for it, but she was enjoying locking herself away to type out the words and disappear back into other worlds. It turned out that was the main part she missed about acting.

She pushed open the door to Michael's office and glanced around at the cool green walls, dark wooden floor and large French doors that led out onto the garden. The sky was grey and heavy, threatening snow which already lay on top of the hills. Frankie had put fairy lights up outside the doors; she put them on as it grew dark and, if Michael was home, it served as a reminder to venture into the kitchen where she'd be waiting with her mother's mince pies and a cup of tea.

On his desk were a few books, mostly about veterinary care but there were also two about architecture. They sat beside a notebook and pen, full of Michael's now familiar scrawled hand-writing, and his laptop. Frankie bent to open the top drawer of the desk and dug her phone from her pocket, beaming that she'd managed to find a dress with pockets.

'I think this is bad luck,' came Michael's voice as he answered.

'I'm pretty sure a phone call doesn't count,' said Frankie, smiling. 'Have you checked your emails?'

'No. Why? Have you broken up with me via email?'

Frankie laughed.

'No!' She sighed, exasperated, searching through the random piles of Post-it notes, pens and note-books in the drawer. 'Where's your planning paper-work?'

'In the folder on the top shelf of the bookcase in my office. Why?'

Tutting to herself, Frankie closed the drawer and moved over to the bookcase.

'Check your email.'

'Okay.'

There was a pause as Michael did as he was told and Frankie found the correct folder, opening it and flicking through the pages inside for the paperwork. She stepped back with a vindicated 'Ha!' and waited for Michael to catch up.

'We got it?' he asked.

'Yup. I've found the paperwork. It's all in order. Just need to send off the final forms and confirm everything.'

'This is incredible,' Michael breathed.

'Did you ever have any doubt?'

'Of course I did! But you didn't, did you?'

'Of course I did,' said Frankie. 'But this just feels right, doesn't it? It always has.'

After a moment of silence, they both screamed in delight down the phone to each other.

'I'll do the forms now.'

'What? No! No, no, no. Come here, right now.'

'But—'

'The forms can wait, Frankie. Come here. I want to marry you.'

Michael had proposed after six months. It was far too early in the relationship, but Frankie had screamed yes and thrown herself into his arms. She'd always known she would marry him. If she didn't think about it too hard, she could tell herself that she'd known the moment she'd met him, in the consultation room of his rural practice. Of course that wasn't true. She hadn't known him, how could she have known she would fall so deeply in love with him?

She wasn't sure when the exact moment had been that she'd known she wanted to marry him. Only that it had been quick. So, when Michael had gotten down on one knee during a weekend break to the West coast of Scotland, the rough sea crashing against the dark rocks as the sun beat down on them, she'd said yes before he'd finished asking the question.

Irene had advised taking a year to plan the wedding, but Frankie didn't want anything big. Who would she invite? Everyone she loved was there, in Edinburgh or in Bekburn. She had everything she needed around her already. With the exception of Michael's brother, which had caused a few problems.

The car, decorated with white ribbons, pulled up at the small car park that led to the private woodland. Michael had found the venue – a client whose dog he'd treated for the last five years knew someone who owned the woods and hired it out for events.

Frankie climbed out of the car in her long ivory wedding dress, her lace sleeves reaching down to her wrists. The chill December wind brushed over her, but she didn't care. Her mother offered her a coat, which she accepted, although her body sang with heat and apprehension. On her feet were white Wellington boots, ready to get covered in mud that the woods had waiting for her.

She scooped up her skirts and walked down the path with her parents, unable to keep the grin from her face as the venue owner met her.

'You're bang on time! Everyone else is here. Are you ready? Just need to speak to the registrar.'

That didn't take long. Frankie and her father signed the appropriate paperwork, the registrar explained how the ceremony would work, although Frankie heard none of it, and then, suddenly, she was taking her parents' arms and approaching the site of the ceremony.

The wedding party was so small that there were only a handful of chairs either side of the aisle, placed carefully in the small clearing, surrounded by tall pines. The smell, even in December, was wonderful. Behind the registrar, at the end of the aisle, was a large Christmas tree, decorated with white lights and silver ornaments. Fairy lights hung around the tree trunks, creating a warm glow in the dark afternoon.

Just in front of the registrar was Michael, standing tall and handsome in his dark suit. He turned and smiled at Frankie, his eyes widening a little, his features softening. Beside him, Jamie grinned and gave Frankie a little wave.

She couldn't smile any more than she was, and she had to hold in a laugh as she practically skipped down the aisle, past Dane and his wife, Sandy and her boyfriend, Jamie's wife and children, and Esme, sitting with her book club, wiping at their eyes with tissues.

The ceremony went in a blur. Frankie knew she said the right words at the right time, but only because Michael smiled and gave her something of a nod. At the end, he winked, and Frankie did her best to stay upright.

They slid rings on each other's cold fingers and kissed, to the applause of the small crowd around them.

Walking back up the aisle, Michael held Frankie's hand and squeezed.

'Hello, wife.' He lifted her chilled hand to his warm lips.

'Hello, husband. You look so incredibly handsome,' Frankie whispered.

'You look stunningly beautiful,' he whispered back.

The venue owner guided them to a little quiet area where they could be alone for a minute. Michael accepted a couple of glasses of champagne and their congratulations.

'To us,' he said, holding up his glass as he passed the other to Frankie. 'To my beautiful wife and the amazing adventure we're about to embark on.'

'And to a whole new charity, a whole new apartment complex complete with veterinary practice for people who find themselves on the streets or sofa surfing,' Frankie said, grinning so hard that her cheeks ached. 'And to my incredible husband whose hugs not only feel like coming home, but who gave me the purpose I'd been searching for all this time.'

They clinked glasses.

'Wow. What are we going to say for the speeches?' Michael asked, watching Frankie sip her champagne.

'Screw the speeches. We're going to dance!'

Michael laughed.

'Dance, and kiss, and go on honeymoon. Then we'll finish all those forms,' he said.

Frankie disagreed with the order, but she didn't say so. Right then, a party with the people she loved the most followed by two weeks alone with her new husband sounded perfect.

'And then the next adventure,' Frankie said, lifting herself up on tiptoes.

'Turns out all I needed was you,' Michael murmured, leaning down to kiss her lips, his warmth spreading through Frankie just as soft Christmas music began playing; their cue to leave that little area and re-join their family and friends as husband and wife.

A LIVING ROOM IN A FARMHOUSE ON THE EDGE OF A SCOTTISH TOWN...

'I call this meeting of the Weird Reading Sisters to order,' said Doreen. 'Is this an official meeting?'

'Well, there's wine,' said Esme, holding up a bottle. The women cheered and raised their mostly empty glasses. Esme went around the room and topped everyone up before sitting back in the armchair. It belonged to Michael and was the same armchair she'd sat on in his flat, Agnes on her lap. Now it was in Michael and Frankie's living room, in the farmhouse. She stroked the arm lovingly, which Agnes took to be an invitation. The cat jumped up into her lap, painfully kneaded her legs and then curled into a ball, purring as Esme rubbed her ears.

'What a wonderful wedding,' said Molly, sitting back into the sofa and closing her eyes. 'And so nice of Michael to let us stay the night. I couldn't have gotten back to the city.'

'One of us would have needed to not drink,' Doreen agreed, taking a gulp of wine. 'Plus we couldn't have stayed up until three in the morning, like this.'

'It's three in the morning?' Faye questioned, looking towards the windows where the heavy curtains shut out the night. 'Witching hour,' she murmured, sipping her wine. 'I wonder why they didn't want to spend their first night together here. It's such a lovely house.'

'They've got the rest of their lives to enjoy this house,' Irene told them, leaning forward to take a mince pie from the coffee table in the middle. They'd eaten so much at the wedding and she'd only put the mince pies out to be a good hostess, but now she couldn't stop looking at them. 'I think it's romantic. Their first night as husband and wife in a hotel suite.'

'I don't think romantic is the word for it,' Doreen murmured.

Both Esme and Irene looked up at her and she tutted.

'Oh, please. Yes, they're your children, but they're also very grown up. My youngest is younger than Frankie and has two children! Where do you think children come from? That's why they wanted a hotel suite.'

Esme and Irene exchanged a glance, the corners of their mouths twitching in a shared smile.

'A grandchild would be nice,' Irene murmured.

'They're obviously capable of creating beautiful things together,' Esme agreed.

'Yes, yes, it's all lovely, but when are we going to talk about what none of us are saying?' said Molly, hiccupping and reaching for a mince pie.

The women stared at her.

'What are we not saying, Mol?' asked Doreen.

Molly shrugged.

'We did a spell from that book, to bring love into Michael's life, and here we are. He's married and happy and in love.' She looked each of them in the eye. 'It worked.'

The women glanced at one another, sucking on their teeth, biting their lips as a silence descended.

'It did. Didn't it,' murmured Faye.

'More than you know,' Esme agreed. She'd been unable to tell her friends about Michael's dreaming of Frankie. It was too much, too personal, especially with Frankie's mother in the room. Esme eyed the mince pies, until she became acutely aware of the silence and the heat of four pairs of eyes on her. She looked up to find her friends staring at her. 'What?'

'Should we go around the group?' Faye asked. 'I can go first.'

The women turned to her. Faye cleared her throat.

'I would like to read a thriller for the next book club. Something with a sexy agent in it. All action and explosions and muscles.'

'I think we can do that,' said Doreen.

They raised their glasses and drank.

'Irene?' Esme asked, refilling their glasses.

'Oh, erm.' Irene shifted in her seat, still new to this. 'Just a happy marriage for Frankie and Michael, I think. And maybe a happy, healthy grandchild. If they want to.'

'That's probably on its way to being done,' Doreen declared, and they all raised their glasses and drank.

Irene refilled their glasses, wobbling a little as she stood.

'Esme?'

'Yes, Esme. What do you want?' asked Molly.

'Want?'

'Hmm.'

'Oh, I'm quite happy, thank you,' said Esme, heat rising across her chest and neck.

'You don't feel lonely at all?' asked Faye.

'Maybe at night?' Molly suggested.

'Especially now that Michael has moved out of the city and married,' added Doreen.

'Some women like being on their own,' Irene pointed out.

Again, all eyes turned on Esme.

She gave it a little thought and then cleared her throat.

'What I want is for my two boys to be happy. And they are.'

'Pshh,' Doreen spat, reaching for a mince pie. 'What about your happiness?'

Esme shifted in her seat.

'I guess it would be nice if Jamie and his family moved back to Scotland...' She trailed off as Doreen raised an eyebrow. 'Fine.' Esme sighed. 'It would be nice to have some company. To have what you have, maybe,' she added to Irene. 'Or something a little less committed, like you and Howard,' she said to Doreen. 'Just a nice man to talk to, to spend time with—'

'To have sex with,' said Molly.

Esme smiled and gave a light shrug.

The women laughed, and Doreen reached into her bag by the side of the sofa.

'Good thing I brought this, then,' she said, pulling out the spell book.

Thank you for reading A Scottish Christmas Dream. I hope you enjoyed Frankie and Michael's story.

If you did, please consider leaving a review wherever you get your books to help other readers find Frankie and Michael.

The Vets On Streets charity is based on the wonderful real-life charity, StreetVet (which is a much better name!).

Please consider supporting them in whatever way you can.

LOOKING FOR YOUR NEXT ROMANCE?

Try the **Christmas At The Manor** trilogy of three novellas,

Digging The Director

and

Let's Skip This Christmas

by Jennifer Nice.

Find your next read at
www.writeintothewoods.com/romance

www.ingramcontent.com/pod-product-compliance
Lightning Source LLC
Chambersburg PA
CBHW050546190726
48283CB00007B/2031